W9-CEA-955

Angelina woke up wrapped in Jeremy's arms, weak from the pleasures of the previous night. She looked at her watch and closed her eyes again. They only had two more full days together— today and tomorrow. What would happen then?

She tried to move from within his arms without disturbing him, but as she shifted away from him, he shifted closer, holding her tighter. She tried again, and the same thing happened. On the third try, low grumbling laughter came from deep in his chest.

"Are you trying to get away?" he asked.

"Yes, I am. And you're wide-awake."

"It's early, and I like holding you."

"Well I have a day planned."

He opened his eyes, "Are you going ashore?"

"We could later, but I have a spa appointment this morning."

"I see. And you were trying to sneak away."

He chuckled, grabbing her firmly by the hips and pulling her against the length of his body.

Books by Yasmin Sullivan

Harlequin Kimani Romance

Return to Love
Love on the High Seas

YASMIN SULLIVAN

grew up in upstate New York and St. Thomas, Virgin Islands, from which her family hails. She moved to Washington, D.C., to attend college and has earned degrees from Howard University and Yale University. As an academic writer, she has published works on by Frederick Douglass, Harriet Jacobs, James Baldwin, Maya Angelou and Ed Bullins, as well as the writing of the Negritude Movement and historical fiction treating emancipation in the Danish West Indies/United States Virgin Islands. She currently lives in Washington, D.C., where she teaches with a focus on African-American and Caribbean literatures. When she isn't teaching, she does creative writing and works on mosaics.

Love on the HIGH SEAS

YASMIN SULLIVAN

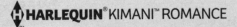

HARLEQUIN® KIMANI™ ROMANCE

If you purchased this book without a cover you should be aware that this book is stolen property. It was reported as "unsold and destroyed" to the publisher, and neither the author nor the publisher has received any payment for this "stripped book."

For my mother, father, brother and grandmother,
who have given me the richness of the human heart;
for Jennie and Tanya, who have been my sister-friends;
for Madeline, Freddie and William, who have shaped my vision of
love; and for Vionette and Lois, who have inspired the romantic in me.

Recycling programs
for this product may
not exist in your area.

ISBN-13: 978-0-373-86331-0

LOVE ON THE HIGH SEAS

Copyright © 2013 by Yasmin Y. DeGout

All rights reserved. The reproduction, transmission or utilization of this work in whole or in part in any form by any electronic, mechanical or other means, now known or hereafter invented, including xerography, photocopying and recording, or in any information storage or retrieval system, is forbidden without written permission. For permission please contact Harlequin Kimani, 225 Duncan Mill Road, Toronto, Ontario M3B 3K9, Canada.

This is a work of fiction. Names, characters, places and incidents are either the product of the author's imagination or are used fictitiously, and any resemblance to actual persons, living or dead, business establishments, events or locales is entirely coincidental.

® and TM are trademarks of Harlequin Enterprises Limited or its corporate affiliates. Trademarks indicated with ® are registered in the United States Patent and Trademark Office, the Canadian Trade Marks Office and in other countries.

For questions and comments about the quality of this book, please contact us at CustomerService@Harlequin.com.

Printed in U.S.A.

Dear Reader,

A poet once said that there's nothing better than having someone with whom to dream. Our dreams then seem more possible, more viable, more workable, more real. Sharing a good romance novel does the same thing. It allows us to dream together, making us kindred spirits, so that love becomes more possible, more viable, more real in our own lives.

I hope that this novel connects us across such a dream. It is the story of Angelina Lewis and Jeremy Bell, whose story is about learning to embrace the possibility of love and accepting the thrill of the sensual side that lives in each of us.

I am already at work on my next romance project, and I would love to hear your thoughts on this book. Please write me at yasminhu@aol.com.

Warm wishes,

Yasmin

Chapter 1

Angelina Lewis fidgeted on the gangway, stuck in line with the horde of other passengers boarding the Palace of the Seas, one of the largest cruise ships on the Atlantic. It was an hour before departure, when the throng had arrived, but the line was moving along quickly.

She might even have found a way to enjoy the short wait if she wasn't sure that at least one more person would measure her against the passport she carried. Instead, the suspense of potential exposure was unnerving her. She couldn't believe that she'd let her sister talk her into this.

Safire had shown up with a suitcase, a ticket and her usual chipper mood, and before Angelina knew what was what, they were in her room packing.

Safire's calm, elliptical eyes followed Angelina as she flew back and forth across the room. Her sister still wore her usual blazer and matching miniskirt—her work attire. She tugged down the skirt as she adjusted herself on the bed, letting her long curls fall across the pillow. Safire's plump cheeks puckered from her smile—one caused by mere amusement or by some thought that was more salacious. Angelina couldn't tell.

"I can't do this." Angelina tore through her closet furiously. "I have work to do. Who'll look after Philly?"

"You have to, or it'll go to waste. I told you. One of my bosses went into labor early, so I can't take off now. You can bring your work with you." Safire sprawled over Angelina's bed observing her distraught search. "Alex and I can take care of Philly and Rose. It's all paid for. Live a little. Please."

Safire flipped open the suitcase she had placed on the bed. "Look, you don't even have to pack. I was all ready to go. It has everything you need, except some shoes, some undies and your toiletries."

"There's barely anything in there."

"You won't need a lot, especially not if you find a sexy man."

Safire winked at her, and Angelina gaped.

"I can't be like you, running around in skimpy nothings." Angelina knew her sister well and could imagine what she'd packed. "No, no. I can't do this. It's a singles cruise. What am I going to do there?"

"Mingle. Get a life. Get you some. Or just lounge, swim in the pool, see the sights. You don't have to do the singles events. It's a regular cruise."

"Okay, let's say I do this. I have to get to the bank, pack my work, pack the suitcase, situate Philly, call the neighbors—"

"It doesn't leave until four o'clock tomorrow. All of that is doable," Safire said. "Here. Take my passport. Put it with the ticket and the cruise information."

"I can't take your passport. We'll just change the passenger information."

"I checked. It's too late to do that. Just use my passport. You're my sister."

"No," said Angelina. "I can't get away with being you."

"Of course you can. Here. Now no more about it."

Angelina shook her head. She'd be calling the cruise line herself in the morning. There would be a fee, but she would just pay it. Her sister had gotten everything else, so she could pay for that.

Now she stood on board the ship just inside the boarding ramp. One of the crew members looked toward her, and she began to hand over the passport once more. It had been too late to change the passenger manifest, so she was Safire Lewis for the next nine days.

"No, ma'am, I don't need your passport. I wanted to give you directions. Do you have your stateroom key?"

"Yes," Angelina answered, "but I wanted to go on deck first to see the departure. Can I do that?"

"Of course. Just follow the left line to the elevators. Six floors up you'll find the least crowded deck right now."

"Thank you."

Angelina shifted her purse and her laptop carry-on from one shoulder to the other and kept step with the line. She looked ahead of her in the line to see how much farther she had to go and found a pair of simmering brown eyes peering back at her. They belonged to a handsome chestnut-brown face that was wearing an intense expression of interest—so intense that she felt naked under the sly perusal.

Angelina flushed, and her cheeks grew hot. Her hand sprang to the buttons lining the front of her dress, checking in case one had come undone. She wasn't sure how long she held his gaze; it seemed an hour but couldn't have been for more than a minute.

A woman behind her bumped against her, and Angelina was startled out of her reverie. She turned briefly to the woman, and by the time she turned back, the man had gone around a corner.

She could have just imagined it. He could have been looking beyond her, or he could have simply seen that she was one of the few other African-Americans there. But perhaps that also made it clear that she was alone. She might need to be a bit more careful, more aware of her surroundings.

"You need to have some fun for a change," Safire had said.

"A singles mixer isn't my idea of fun right now. I have a semester starting soon. I have an article I haven't finished. I have—"

"You have to get a life is what," Safire said and then laughed. "When was the last time you had nookie?"

"Now, listen here. I might need to talk to you about—"

"Oh, no. Don't start in on me. I have a life. And I enjoy it just fine. This is about you. Relax a little. Meet some people. See some places."

Angelina could tell that her younger sister was treading gently to spare her sensibilities, and it was just as well. Her sister had a mouth on her that could make a sailor blush. She envied her sister's freedom, but for Angelina herself, a bit of reading next to the ocean would be a wonderful break. And with the passport fiasco, laying low seemed like a good idea.

When she stepped off the elevator six stories up, the line was gone. People were relaxing in lounge chairs and looking over the railing at the Port of Miami. She found a spot on the banister for the departure, wondering if she'd feel the ship move or if it was simply too large.

Being on deck made what was happening real. She—Angelina Lewis—was actually on a cruise ship going somewhere.

When the horn sounded the departure call, Angelina was exhilarated. She didn't feel the push off, but she could see the landscape begin to shift as they pulled out of the harbor. She held on to the rail and leaned over, gauging their movement from the receding pier and leaving behind the workaday world as a dark blue expanse opened before her.

For a moment, she forgot about her lists and her obligations. For a moment, she let it all sink in and felt herself enjoy the rush.

She stepped down from the rail and lifted her laptop bag to her shoulder again. She was already smiling when she turned around and found herself again locked in the distant gaze of sensuous brown eyes.

He was across the deck with a small group of other Black men, and he was staring at her, trapping her against the rail. Under his gaze, Angelina felt goose bumps run up her back. Her nipples tightened against her bra, and butterflies began to churn in her stomach. His eyes were trained on her, sensual ebony ovals above angular cheekbones and a rugged jawline. He smiled in her direction with thick, lush lips.

Angelina's hand fluttered to her chest, and she took a deep breath. Was he looking at her? She glanced to each side. On one there was a family of five still looking toward the shoreline; on the other was a group of teenagers making a lively ruckus. She turned back. It must be her. She felt a tingle in the pit of her stomach and had to stop herself from turning away and fleeing.

He was leaning on the railing with his foot cocked up on one of the lounge chairs in self-assured ease. His elbows rested at his sides atop the rail, and like everything about his pose, his cool confidence suggested that he was out of her league.

He had on a short-sleeved white Oxford shirt that was tucked into pleated blue slacks. The breeze fluttered his shirt along his firm arms up to his broad shoulders, and his top buttons opened to a peek at his hard chest. He was talking with his friends, but all the while he was looking her way.

The brashness of his scrutiny sent shivers through Angelina's body, and her insides buzzed with nervous energy. As self-conscious as she was under his open gaze, something in those eyes made her pulse skip. She had never had such a visceral reaction to anyone before and hoped that it couldn't be read in her features. She pressed her palm against her midriff to calm herself but had to look away.

Angelina had been called her sister's name all afternoon.

Now, on an impulse, she decided to be a little like her baby sis. She took a breath and turned back to the simmering brown eyes and met their gaze, deliberately staring back with an audacious smile on her lips.

She was startled that she was being so brazen.

He seemed to hold her gaze, just as he did before, but nothing else changed. Then, when one of his friends said something, he turned toward the speaker and laughed, breaking his link with her. She certainly couldn't pull it off the way Safire could. So much for the attempt.

Angelina shifted the load on her shoulder and stepped from the railing. Unfortunately, her laptop bag had gotten wedged between the rungs of the railing and toppled her back. She unhooked the bag and launched herself from the banister. No, she certainly couldn't pull off what Safire could.

Had he seen her fumble? Embarrassed, she looked toward the warm brown eyes, but the face that held them was directed elsewhere. Well, she was no Safire. She didn't know what had gotten into her in the first place.

She walked to the elevator, pulled out her key and went to find her cabin.

Angelina's stateroom had everything she would have expected and more, including a balcony on the water. And luckily, she wasn't sharing; she had an oasis all to herself. The first thing on her list was unpacking before dinner, and her suitcase had been delivered so she had only to plop it on the footrest to begin.

The pieces she'd added were on top, so she pulled out a couple of capris, a couple of skirts, a few blouses, a dress and some light tops to go over whatever nonsense Safire had packed for herself. And thank goodness. Safire's clothes were much as she expected.

There were several cocktail dresses, all low-cut and thigh-high. Angelina couldn't imagine herself strutting around in them. The shorts were okay, but Safire had packed skimpy tank tops and racerback T-shirts to go with them. The skirts were all mini and the tops were off-the-shoulder blouses or camisoles. Even the nightclothes she'd packed were sheer, midthigh numbers.

No wonder the case was only half-full when Safire brought it. Everything in it was tiny—just as she'd expected. The last piece of clothing she pulled out was Safire's swimsuit. Such a pity she hadn't remembered her own. She could ball up Safire's bikini and make it disappear inside her fist.

Angelina stood in front of the closet taking inventory. She didn't have enough of her own stuff, so she would have to make do with Safire's pieces. She might have to get another swimsuit on the ship and perhaps a couple of oversize T-shirts to sleep in.

She hadn't budgeted for extra clothes—at least not at what they would cost in floating boutiques. The light coverups she'd brought would supplement the dresses and tank tops, and she didn't plan to go to many events, so she should be okay. After all, it was a cruise. She could be a little like her sister for a little while. She probably wouldn't see anyone here again in life.

This made her think again of those warm brown eyes. What had she been thinking trying to send a signal from across the deck? He probably thought she was a loon. No, he probably wasn't giving her a second thought at all. He could have been looking at the horizon the whole time. In any case, there were several thousand people on the ship. Chances of running into him again didn't seem great, a fact that made her feel both disappointed and relieved.

Angelina turned to the rest of the suitcase and her carry-on—her work. She set up her laptop on the table and piled around it the books and papers she'd brought. She also pulled out all the cruise information: the docking sched-

ule, the brochure for singles, coupons for the tours and a
spa day, a separate booklet describing the ship's amenities,
pamphlets for events and movies.

The next thing to do was to find a place for dinner; she
didn't want to change, so nothing fancy. She found a café-
style restaurant and had a sandwich. Then she went back to
her room and called to check in at home. Safire was there,
and all was well. She started to tell her sister a thing or
two about packing such outrageous clothing, but she gave
it a second thought. Safire wasn't actually packing for *her*
when she'd made those selections, so it didn't make sense
to accuse her of anything willful.

The rest of the evening she was going to lounge on
the balcony and read. That, however, didn't last long. She
started Ellory Patterman's history of the involvement of
Black women in the World War I effort, and enjoying the
book as she was, she drifted into sleep. Angelina woke up
a couple of hours later to find her book on the floor and
her neck stretched precariously to one side.

She got up and went into her room to change for bed
but had only Safire's short, silky nightgowns. There was
nothing to be done about it right then, so she put one on
and crawled into bed. For a few minutes, she watched the
cruise ship's information station on television, but before
long, she clicked the television off. It was a little early, but
she was tired; she'd been tired for some time, and the luxury
of the space let her give in to what she needed most—rest.

If nothing else, she would get to relax a bit over the next
nine days. She might even be able to take her sister's advice
and let loose a little. There could be a little Safire in her yet.

She curled up in bed, letting herself sink into the cool,
crisp sheets. Perhaps it was the enchantment of being
aboard a ship on the way to the Caribbean, or perhaps it
was the sumptuous feel of the gown she had on, but she
drifted off thinking of a warm pair of brown eyes.

Chapter 2

Jeremy Bell had noticed her before she'd even stepped onto the gangway. She was behind his group in the line to board the ship, and she was gorgeous. He could hardly keep from staring at her and hoped that she was one of the members of the singles cruise. She seemed to be. She didn't seem to be with any of the people around her.

She had on a casual yellow sundress and strappy sandals with low wooden heels. The dress was simple enough, but it didn't fully hide the voluptuous curves of her body. When the ocean breeze caught it, he could see the succulent shape of her buttock and the heavy sway of her ripe breasts.

There was something hesitant about her stance, an ongoing inquiry in her expression. She had probably never been on a cruise before. The uncertainty gave her a vulnerable quality that drew his gaze to her even more.

He lost her around a bend, but he was delighted to find that they'd been guided to the same deck for the departure. While he chatted with his friends across the deck, he got a look at her as she hung over the railing, delight and excitement written over her expression.

That, and the way her garment fluttered around her, made his own body react. And he hadn't even met her yet. He was getting ahead of himself, so he settled against the railing to cool down and enjoy the departure with his friends.

They might tease him for trying to talk to a woman on the first day, but he still intended to go over and introduce himself once they were underway. If he didn't, he might lose her in the multitude of people aboard the Palace of the Seas.

When he found her looking back at him, he was pleased, but not surprised. He was in his early thirties, and he still had it going on. For a while she looked away, and he was a little concerned. That wasn't usually the reaction he got from women. He actually sighed in relief when she turned back to him, smiling at him from the banister. That was more like it.

Of course, that was when he lost her. He'd turned to Alistair, who was joking about being the odd man out, and when he turned back she was gone.

He went to three singles functions that night to see if she'd come out to any of them. He took time out to have dinner with his boys—Alistair, Myron and Rudy—at the singles reception in the Senator's Quarters. Then he ditched them to check out a couple of the smaller singles mixers—the one in the Luau Bar and the one in the Messenger Lounge. He didn't see her and had no way of knowing if he'd missed her.

If she wasn't there on the singles cruise, he had no real way to find her again. There were thousands of people on the ship. That's when he remembered the brochure. He pulled it out and rummaged through the pages. Each of them had had to submit a bio and picture for it, and it had come a couple of days before they were set to depart.

Unfortunately, there were dozens of pages of singles listings, and not everyone had sent in a picture. But there weren't that many African-American women in the lineup, either. He found one that seemed to be her. The picture was small, so he couldn't be sure. She was wearing a bikini and waving toward shore from the back of a motorboat. Her name was Safire Lewis, and she was twenty-three, hailing from North Miami. The woman he saw seemed to be older than twenty-three, but then women never told the truth on these things anyway. Right?

Safire Lewis was extroverted and outgoing. She liked swimming and jazz clubs, and she was looking for a man who thought he could tame her urges with tender loving care. She described her style as sophisticated but a bit risqué, and she defined herself as a sensual woman who knew what she wanted and wasn't afraid to get it—a little rambunctious but genial, sometimes saucy but always sweet.

She was looking forward to the singles cruise so that she could relax, kick back and meet some great guys. Her turn-ons were broad shoulders, confidence and someone who knew how to have a good time. Jeremy thought he fit that description. To describe herself in five words or less, she wrote "naughty and nice."

It didn't say much more than that, but that was more than enough.

Jeremy looked back at the picture. Her description of herself turned him on as much as seeing her had done. It made him more determined than ever to find her again the next day, when they would be at sea.

Easier said than done, however. The ship had fourteen decks, twenty restaurants, five spas, four movie theaters, gardens, pools, a casino, a carnival, a shopping district, a sports zone and numerous bars, lounges and cafés.

"You're looking for whom?" Alistair asked.

"A woman I saw in line yesterday."

"And you expect to find her how?"

"I think she's listed in the singles brochure. I'm going to scout out the singles events."

"I'll go with you to the singles stuff," Myron said.

"Me too," Rudy said.

"I, on the other hand, will be at the pool." Alistair wasn't there for the singles mixers; he had a partner back home.

He'd come to relax and enjoy. "I'll meet you guys for lunch. Where?"

They were in Myron's stateroom, and he picked up the booklet for the ship. "Okay. We have about thirty pages of options here."

The other men laughed.

"Is there a singles luncheon venue today?" Rudy asked.

"Oh, joy," Alistair said with a note of sarcasm.

Myron picked up the singles brochure. "In fact, there are three."

"Pick one," Jeremy said.

Myron shrugged. "The Onyx sounds good."

"The Onyx it is. One o'clock."

Jeremy, Myron and Rudy did a round of the singles events listed for that morning. Myron had started talking to a woman at the Pool and Cabana mixer, so they left him behind and headed to the Café mixer. She wasn't there, and they didn't want to go to the Date for the Day event, so Rudy left him to join Alistair, and Jeremy continued on alone.

Before heading to the Onyx, he stopped at the concierge to see if he could get Safire Lewis's cabin number or telephone, which turned out to be the same thing. He tried calling the number they gave him but got no answer. At least he knew that if it was her—if the woman he saw was Safire Lewis—he could hope to reach her by phone. That much discovered, he joined his boys for lunch, still keeping an eye out for her.

He called her again before dinner—no luck. He called again after dinner—eureka.

"Hello."

He had no idea what her voice sounded like.

"Hi, I'm trying to reach Safire Lewis."

There was a pause on the other end. "Yes, this is she."

"My name is Jeremy Bell, and I think I saw you when I

was boarding the ship. I was wondering if you might want to get together for coffee or dancing or—"

"Who is this?" she asked.

Jeremy laughed out loud.

"I'm sorry. That's a fair question. I'm on the singles cruise, and I think I saw you when we boarded. You had on a yellow dress. I wanted to meet you."

"And you were wearing?"

"What was I wearing? I had on a white shirt and blue pants, I think. Let me check my closet. Yes, that was it. I thought you might have noticed me, too."

"I remember you. But how did you get my name, my number?"

"After looking for you all day, I checked the singles listing. Luckily, there aren't that many Black women on this cruise, so I took a chance that you were the one I saw."

"Oh." There was a pause.

"Look, you probably already have plans for tonight because it's New Year's Eve, but if you don't, maybe we can meet at one of the mixers."

"I hadn't actually planned on going out tonight. I brought some work with me and was in for the night. But maybe..."

He could hear her hesitation, but at least she was thinking about it.

"I had planned on going to the Peacock Lounge for their New Year's Eve party. Maybe we could meet there."

He didn't get a response right away.

"I'm not sure. Let me see how much I get done, and I'll consider."

"Well, no pressure. I'll be there, and if you don't recognize me, I'm sure I'll recognize you. I hope you can come."

"I'll see," she said.

It was clear that she didn't want to commit, so he decided not to push it.

"It would be great to meet you, so I'll keep a lookout."

"Okay, then."

"Goodbye."

Clearly, he hadn't made the impression he thought he'd made. When she looked back at him and smiled, he thought that they'd connected. Now she seemed unsure if she wanted to meet him.

To be fair, she didn't know him from Adam; he could be a serial murderer. She seemed more cautious than her bio had led him to believe. That, or she was swamped with something for work. Or she simply wasn't that interested in him from what she saw. He had no way of knowing.

At least she remembered him. And she might come tonight. He wasn't sure what he would be doing until he spoke to her. In fact, he probably would have rung in the New Year at one of the sports bars with his boys if he hadn't spoken to her. Now, he had time to change and catch up with the guys to let them know his new plans.

He met up with Alistair and Rudy at a sports bar around ten o'clock. Myron had a date with the woman that he'd met at the Pool and Cabana mixer, and Jeremy would be meeting them in the Peacock Lounge at eleven.

"I'll be back before twelve-thirty if she doesn't show."

"She'll show," said Alistair. "Hottie that you are."

"Thanks for the vote of confidence."

When he got to the Peacock Lounge, he was given a mask made of peacock feathers. He didn't know that everyone would have them on, and he hoped he could still tell who she was. At least there wouldn't be that many choices.

The champagne was already flowing from towers of crystal glasses arranged on silver platters. An elaborate ball was rigged to drop, and the countdown was already ticking down on a monitor. Whistles and party favors were piled up on tables skirting the room.

He found Myron and his date on the dance floor and nodded to his friend. Myron had a thick frame and wore a loose yellow panama shirt with a pair of brown slacks. He had tracked Jeremy's entrance with one lazy eye and nodded at Jeremy over his date's shoulder.

After a couple of songs, they came over, and Myron introduced him to Verniece. She had a pleasant smile and seemed completely unassuming. Her tall, full figure matched Myron's thickness, and even her yellow skirt set with French dots blended with Myron's attire. The two seemed evenly paired.

The three chatted for a while, and then he left the couple to enjoy their evening together, wandering over to the array of cheeses and breads. Nearing midnight he began to get a little disappointed, but he still held out. Safire had been noncommittal, but she at least seemed to consider his invitation. He would give her until half past midnight, maybe even longer, because she seemed well worth the wait.

He recognized her the moment she hit the doorway, and what he saw made his body pulse. She had on a strapless red cocktail dress that hit her midthigh and hugged every delicious curve of her body. Over that she wore a sheer red wrap with a floral burnout pattern. It was almost as long as the dress, but so translucent that it hid nothing of her shapely curves.

When she stepped down into the lounge, he saw that she had on black pumps that showed off her taut calves and supple rear. As she rounded the banister, he walked toward her.

Her face was partially hidden by the peacock mask, but the pretense of anonymity only made her look sexier than ever. Her lips were red and smiling, and she'd piled her hair on top of her head in cascading black curls.

She seemed a little hesitant in a way that made her seem vulnerable, but then she hadn't seen him as yet, and she didn't know him.

"Safire?"

"Jeremy?"

He lifted his mask so that she could see his face. "Yes, it's me. I'm glad that you could make it. When it got close to midnight, I began to worry."

"I'm glad I made it, too, and with two minutes to spare." She was looking at the countdown on the monitor.

He took her hand and led her toward the dance floor. He couldn't help smiling. When they got near the center of the floor, he didn't let her hand go. Knowing that she wasn't afraid to get what she wanted, he held her hand within his, playing his fingers over hers. It was sensual and erotic touching the fingers of a masked stranger.

They just looked at each other for several moments, and then the crowd around them started counting down the seconds. That was when he knew he would kiss her.

When the count got to ten everyone joined in, and the chant rose around them. They simply stared at each other through peacock-feathered masks, waiting. Suddenly, the Happy New Year call went up and the ball dropped, accompanied by an explosion of silver confetti and streams of colored balloons.

Jeremy stepped to Safire, put his arms around her and brought his lips to hers. For a moment, they lingered that way, lips poised, close to each other. Then he touched his lips to hers, possessing her and drawing her body against his.

At first she was still, not willing to give in to the moment. But as he continued to move his lips over hers, they softened underneath his, and her hands came up to his shoulders, pressing lightly against him.

He gripped her hips harder and pulled her flush against him, parting her lips. Her mouth opened for him, and he slid his tongue into the sweet wetness of her. Her grip on his shoulders tightened, and her mouth widened, letting him in. She stirred in his embrace, and her arms came up to surround his shoulders and then his neck. Her fingers at his nape sent a quiver through his body and heat into his loins.

Their tongues began to explore, and he was seared by the heat of her body. Her chest heaved against his with each breath, and he wrapped his arms more fully around her.

He had no idea how long they remained locked together, but when he opened his eyes, they were calf-deep in balloons, and the silver confetti in her hair made her look like an angel.

As he looked at her, her cheeks flushed. She took a breath and stepped back from him, straightening her body and dusting the confetti from her shoulders. She looked around them nervously.

"I don't know what got into me," she said.

He could see the embarrassment written over her as she continued to pick the confetti from her clothing. It made him smile.

"Happy New Year," he said.

She smiled and stopped fussing over the confetti.

"Happy New Year to you, too."

"It's time for champagne."

"Oh, none for me. I hadn't planned to stay, really. I just wanted to come welcome in the New Year and say hello."

"You can't leave so soon. You just got here. Give me the first dance of the New Year."

"I'm sorry. I really should go. I have some work I'd planned to get done tonight."

Jeremy couldn't help the disappointment he was starting to feel.

"How about tomorrow? Can we meet for lunch?"

"That would be—" She stopped. "I'm on a tour tomorrow when we stop at Nassau."

"Have you ever been to the Bahamas?"

"No, but I've heard it's beautiful."

"Then you have to go see Nassau," he said. "My friends

and I planned to disembark as well, but just to do some shopping and hit the beach. You enjoy the tour."

She smiled and turned to go, but he wasn't giving up that quickly.

"Wait. What about dinner?"

She turned back to him. "That sounds good. Will other singles be there?"

Jeremy hadn't planned on a group for dinner, but he sensed it would make her more comfortable.

"Yes, we can meet at one of the singles buffets and go from there. I still have your number. I'll call and leave a message when we figure out which one."

"That'll be fine. I'm sorry I have to run."

Jeremy wanted to take hold of her and kiss her again, even if it was a kiss good-night. But something told him not to go that quickly. He simply smiled at her, and she smiled back before turning toward the door.

After the fire of the kiss, Jeremy had hoped that they would end up in each other's arms tonight. Instead, he nodded toward Myron on the dance floor and decided to make his way back to the sports bar to find Alistair and Rudy.

He couldn't wait to see Safire again, to feel her in his arms again. If she wasn't afraid to get what she wanted, he had to find a way to let her know that he was it. But that would have to wait until tomorrow night.

Chapter 3

Angelina was getting dressed in one of her sister's cocktail gowns, just as she had the night before. She hadn't planned to go to a New Year's Eve party, but when the owner of those warm brown eyes called her, as surprised as she was, she couldn't resist the possibility of seeing him again, this time up close.

She'd spent most of yesterday on her balcony, reading, leaving only for meals and to wander briefly around one of the decks. That had made it even more exciting to have an invitation to get out that night.

Still, what was she getting herself into? Did she want to get herself into anything, or did she want to stick with the plan to lay low? Plus, after she had given him her best Safire-like smile, she didn't know what he might expect. She had put her foot in her mouth, so to speak.

Last night, she had gotten all dressed up, putting one of her cover-ups over one of her sister's short dresses. It had made her feel sexy, but maybe it'd looked too sexy. She couldn't decide. She hadn't even been sure she should go; in fact, she'd dawdled until it was almost too late. Finally, she had decided that it couldn't hurt to go for a little while—just to meet him.

She couldn't have known she would end up in the most sensual kiss of her life. And with a stranger, no less. It seemed that some of her sister was getting into her after all, and she'd decided to leave before something else happened, something she wasn't prepared for.

Today, she'd spent the sunlight hours in Nassau and would forever be enchanted with the Bahamas. The tour had started with a driving visit to the forts and a stop at the Pirate Museum. Then they'd gone to Predator Lagoon to see sharks and barracuda. They'd also had a walking visit of the Ardastra Gardens with its "marching" flamingoes. Lunch had been in the shopping district, and those who didn't want to get wet stayed to shop. Angelina went for the water. She'd brought a change of clothes and had just worn her shorts over Safire's bikini.

At the next stop, she'd petted and fed the dolphins, and at the stop after that, followed the snorkeling trail to the Rainbow Reef, where the sand was white and warm, and the water was so crystal clear she could see down to the bottom of the ocean floor. After the snorkeling, she'd swum and then relaxed on the beach in the sun. If she got nothing else from the whole trip, that day had made it worthwhile.

But the tour hadn't been over. After she'd changed into her extra set of clothes, they were dropped off for an hour-long glass-bottom boat tour before the safari took them back to the ship.

She'd been kept busy all day, but she hadn't forgotten about that night. The phone was blinking when she got in, and when she checked the message, she found out that Jeremy Bell's group would be meeting at seven o'clock to have dinner at the Starlight, an open-air restaurant. She barely had time to wash and dry her hair and get dressed.

She was wearing Safire's turquoise dress this time. It was a thin, knit material of some kind and was as revealing as the other one—as they all were—but she had a short, silver eyelet bolero jacket to put over it. The jacket was made of a satiny material that could go with most evening pieces, which was why she'd brought it. It might be too warm, but it was worth it to have a little coverage on top.

She didn't have a lot of time to blow-dry her hair, so she

pulled it back in a ponytail and added a silver bow. Her skin was still warm from the sun, but she added a little makeup and finished off with her strappy silver two-inch sandals.

She was going to a fair amount of trouble just for dinner, but she couldn't deny her excitement. Of course, she hadn't gotten any work done that day, which was a problem. She would make up for it tonight and tomorrow.

At six-forty, her phone rang. It could only be Jeremy Bell.

"I was just about to head out the door," she said.

"I thought I might walk you to the restaurant."

"Making sure I don't ditch out, huh?"

They both chuckled.

"No," he answered, "but definitely wanting to see you again."

"I wasn't sure I'd make it on time, but I'm actually ready. Hey, since I was heading out anyway, why don't I just meet you at an elevator or in front of the restaurant? Where is it?"

Jeremy laughed for a moment. "See, I've actually figured that out. That's why I thought I would meet you, so you wouldn't have to. And I'm about five doors down from you at this point."

Angelina poked her head out of the door and found Jeremy's tall, broad-shouldered figure striding toward her down the hall. He had a cell phone to his ear.

They both laughed.

Angelina smiled and waved. Something had gotten into her mood tonight. She was smiling and being a bit silly, but she liked it.

When he got to her door, she took the phone from her ear and greeted him.

"Hello. Let me just put the phone down and get my pocketbook."

He stood just inside the doorway and waited, a crooked

smile on his face and a glint in his eye, watching her all the while.

When she came back to the door, ready, he held his arm out for her.

She gave him a skeptical look. "So chivalry isn't dead, after all." She chuckled and took his arm, unable to conquer her giddiness. They headed past the nearby elevators to the far ones.

"These are closer to the Starlight," Jeremy said.

"Where is your stateroom? Are you on this floor?"

"No, I'm two floors up. I'll show you sometime."

He smiled at her. She couldn't tell whether or not he was being saucy, but just in case, she said, "Don't they all look the same, anyway?"

"More or less."

"I actually did think I would be late. I should have gotten your number, just in case."

With his free hand, he fished in this pocket. "Here, take one of my cards. This one has my cell phone number on it, and that's the phone I carry."

"Thank you."

By the time they got to the eleventh floor, only one other couple was on the elevator. Jeremy took her chin and brought her lips to his, kissing her lightly.

"Hello again."

His gesture was so sweet and so gentle that it stopped Angelina in her tracks. She couldn't help smiling back.

"Hi."

She waited for him to do something else, but he just smiled at her.

"You're in a strange mood tonight, aren't you?" she asked.

"Only because I'm with you again."

"I'm in a strange mood, too. I don't know if it was kissing a dolphin—"

"You kissed a dolphin?"

"Yes, the tour let us play with them, feed them. I got my picture taken kissing one. I snorkeled. I swam. It was all wonderful."

"You look like you're glowing. You look beautiful, Safire."

"Thank you, Jeremy."

He slipped his hand into hers as they exited the elevator on the fourteenth floor. The familiarity between them made it seem as though they had been seeing each other for a while, but the actual newness of his hand in hers sent a thrill through Angelina's body.

In the atrium of the Starlight, she was introduced to Jeremy's friend Myron and Verniece, Myron's date. The four of them would be dining together at a table of eight, so they would be meeting four new people. These turned out to be a newlywed couple from Idaho and an older couple from Scranton, Pennsylvania.

Over drinks, they met one another and talked about the New Year's Eve events they'd attended. Angelina blushed when she remembered her kiss with Jeremy and was even more embarrassed when he noticed this. He put a consoling arm over the back of her chair and rubbed her shoulder with his thumb. It sent a shiver through her body that she tried to hide.

They also talked about what they had seen of the Bahamas that day.

"We went out with the dolphins, did the powerboat ride and spent the afternoon on the beach," Drake, the newlywed, said.

"Did you kiss a dolphin?" Jeremy asked Drake's wife. Angelina saw the humor in his eyes and swatted him playfully.

"I sure did," Rosalie answered. "It was better than kissing a frog."

"Or a man," Angelina added, and the two women laughed.

Jeremy looked at her with surprise and with a challenge in his eyes that said he would be proving her wrong very soon.

"I went on the daylong tour, and it was glorious," Angelina said. "I think we did everything there was to do in Nassau. I was gone all day. I loved it."

Angelina stopped when she realized she was gushing. She really did need to get out more. She laughed at herself, and Jeremy turned to her.

She waved away the inquiry and went on chatting.

"What did you guys do, Verniece?"

The woman was hanging on Myron's shoulder and looked at him. Angelina could tell that she shouldn't have asked.

"No, no. You don't have to tell us if it's too scandalous," Angelina said.

The table laughed.

"We did get to the pool for a while," Verniece offered. "And we had lunch in the Coco Lounge. But other than that, we stayed in."

Angelina turned to Myron and Jeremy. "Weren't you two with other gentlemen?"

"Alistair and Rudy," Myron said. "They decided to go to one of the singles lounges for dinner and let the couples be by themselves."

Once dinner arrived, the conversation quieted down a little. It turned out that the older couple was used to cruising, so they gave some advice about when to arrive and how to get discounts.

After dinner, Jeremy, Angelina, Myron and Verniece lingered in the atrium of the Starlight, trying to decide on the next thing they would do.

"I really should be getting back," said Angelina. "I was

gone all day and didn't do anything I brought with me to get done."

Jeremy put his palm against her back. It sent another shiver through her body that she tried once again to hide.

"Come dancing with us, Safire. You don't have to stay long."

"Dancing sounds great," Verniece said.

"There's a place called the Silhouette Lounge," Jeremy said. "They have desserts, drinks, dancing. Please."

"For a little while," Angelina said.

When they got to the Silhouette Lounge, Angelina picked up immediately on the romantic theme; it was a hangout for couples, replete with low lighting, soft seating and slow music.

Myron and Verniece stopped at the bar for drinks, but Jeremy drew her onto the dance floor, slid his hands around her waist and began to sway.

Angelina's palms came up to his chest. She thought it would keep a polite distance between them; instead, she could feel how hard his body was through his panama shirt, and that made the gesture seem even more intimate.

Angelina let herself rock to the music—something slow and Italian. As he held her closer, she moved her arms to his shoulders, bringing her chest against his. The sensation sent a tingle through her body, and she it hoped wasn't noticeable.

Angelina was five-eleven, and in her two-inch heels, she was almost Jeremy's height. When he lowered his head just a bit, it brought their cheeks together. She rested her head against his, closed her eyes and finally just let herself enjoy their dance.

The next song was in Spanish and just as intoxicating. When she opened her eyes briefly, she found that she had slipped her arms around his neck, not remembering when she had done so. When she turned to him, he was smiling at her.

"I love dancing with you this way," he said.

"It's been a while since I've danced like this."

"You're not rusty at all. I love the way your body feels against mine."

"Thank you." She didn't know what else to say. His low bass voice in her ear sent goose bumps down her back and made her body twitch. She couldn't tell whether this was apparent or not.

The next song was in Portuguese, she thought, something of a tango. She snuggled closer to his shoulder and swayed with his movement. His hands tightened around her back, bringing her body closer to his.

The thin knit of her sister's gown did almost nothing to shield Angelina from the intimate contact of Jeremy's body. She could feel his manhood pressing against her hip, and she sucked in a breath. He only held her closer and moved himself along her until he was nestled at the center of her body. Her sex started to throb, and her breath became heavier.

As he swayed against her, his body rubbed against her center and sent delicious prickles through her sex and into her breasts. Of their own volition, her hips tilted forward, bringing her into greater contact with the onslaught of his manhood. She caught herself and stopped the vulgar thrust, but she could feel herself growing damp, growing needy. Her arms gripped his neck tighter, and she bent her face toward his shoulder, not wanting to be seen.

Jeremy left one hand pressed against her back and drew the other up to her nape. The gentle fingers exploring her neck made her shiver and twist in his embrace, and the sensations running through her body made her gasp for air. Her mouth was already open when he turned to her and found her lips with his own, pressing his tongue deep inside.

A murmur escaped her and was trapped by his mouth. She hoped that he hadn't heard it over the music, but in response, he pressed even closer to her and held her in place, running his chest against her breasts and his manhood along her sex. Angelina pulled herself from his lips as the sensations poured over her. Her core throbbed, wanting more, and she winced, sucking in her breath. She knew he could hear her, but she couldn't help it.

He put his lips to her ear. "Your body has been responsive to my touch all evening, Safire."

Angelina was mortified that he had noticed. She didn't know what to say, and she could barely think with his deep voice sending shivers down her spine.

"Let me come back to your room with you. Let me make love to you."

Angelina stepped back, unsure how to answer. Her body was crying out to be loved by this man, but she wasn't Safire. She didn't just go to bed with men. They were still strangers. And she wasn't that daring.

"I—I don't think I can. I don't really know you yet."

All she really knew was how good he made her feel. She was still catching her breath just from his touch and his body. For once, she wished she was Safire. But she wasn't. She wasn't ready for this.

"I can't. Really." She wanted to, but she couldn't bring herself to do it—to walk back to her room with a stranger and… "I can't."

Jeremy seemed a bit confused and definitely let down. He sighed heavily, conceding to her answer.

"Okay. Get to know me tomorrow. We go to St. Thomas. I wanted to do a bit of shopping. Why don't we go together? Shop, have lunch, get to know each other."

"Okay, if I'm not booked for a tour. I can't remember."

She laughed at herself, and he joined in, breaking the tension between them.

"I need to be going, anyway," she said. "How about if I call you when I get back to my room and let you know?"

"Let me walk you."

"No, no. I know the way from here."

In fact, she didn't, but she could find it. She just didn't trust herself alone in her room with him. As much as her body was turned on, anything could happen. Her hesitancy registered, and he let it go.

"Call me as soon as you get back."

"I will."

He kissed her good-night. The look of desire in his eyes was palpable and made her catch her breath. She had to turn away before she said something she couldn't retract. She hurried to the elevator and pressed the button for her floor.

What was she doing? She had a beautiful man who wanted to come to her room and make love to her, and she had said no. Was she being reasonable, or was she just being afraid? She didn't know, but she had to figure it out and soon.

She got to her room and checked the schedule that Safire had given her. She wasn't booked into a tour of St. Thomas, and they would be there two days. She checked the cruise guide and found a couple of things she would like to do, but they could wait for the second day.

She pulled out his card—Jeremy Bell.

"Hi, it's me."

"I'm glad. I was about to come looking for you." He chuckled.

"I had to look through the brochure to see if there was anything else I wanted to do in St. Thomas. I'm not booked for a tour, but I wanted to go to Coral World and ride the submarine and see some of the castles and..."

He was laughing before she finished.

"What?"

"You don't get out much, do you?"

"Maybe I don't. And who knows when I'll get back to St. Thomas?"

"I'll bring you there on our honeymoon. How's that?"

She could play, too.

"Maybe I want to see Hawaii on our honeymoon. Betcha didn't think about that."

They were both laughing.

"Okay," he said. "Anything you want to do in St. Thomas is fine with me. Just save us a couple of hours on one day to do some shopping. Deal?"

"Deal. What time should we meet?"

"Well, since you want to see the whole island, we should get an early start. How about we meet at eight-thirty for breakfast and disembark at nine?"

"I'll figure out an itinerary for us and let you know in the morning."

"Let's meet in the State Room for breakfast," he suggested.

"I'll see you then."

Angelina hung up feeling elated. It was so easy to be playful with him on the phone. It was up close and personal that it got a bit iffy. She turned on her phone to check in at home. Safire was there again, as promised, and things were going well. She could relax a bit.

If only she could relax. Her body still buzzed from Jeremy's touch and, without her consent, it still wanted more. There was nothing to do but play it by ear. She knew she was being a bit conservative, but she needed to know something about the man before she bedded down with him. And who knew how long that would take?

She giggled to herself as she changed into one of Safire's risqué nighties. Maybe tomorrow she would know enough. It wasn't likely, but she could dream.

Chapter 4

Jeremy had gotten up at seven. It was too early to be getting up, but it gave him an hour in the gym. And that early, he almost had the place to himself, except for Alistair, who was a workout fanatic.

The two had laughed when he had come in to find Alistair on the elliptical machine. But it gave him the chance to update his friend on his new romance and let Alistair know that he'd be gone for the day.

"No, we haven't *done* anything yet."

"Uh-oh. Are you losing your touch? It never takes you this long. Hey, Myron said you got tongue action on the first night. What's happened?"

"Myron has a big mouth. And nothing's happened. Maybe I just want to take it a little slower this time."

"Uh, no," Alistair said and laughed. "Maybe she does."

"Okay, so she does. But I'm liking it this way, too."

"That means you've been bitten by the love bug."

Jeremy put down the forty-pound weight he was lifting and looked at his friend. "Maybe. Too soon to tell."

Alistair raised his eyebrows. *Maybe* said a lot, at least for Jeremy.

Actually, Safire wasn't turning out to be anything like her description—except that she was hot as hell. She'd probably been lying on her application like all the singles— height, age, weight. He chuckled to himself.

Only Safire didn't have to lie. He was even more attracted to who she really was than to the racy profile she'd submitted. He was more intrigued by Safire herself. He could also tell that underneath her controlled demeanor there really was a fiery, sensual woman. He wanted her to come out and play.

He had to admit this much: had they simply gone to bed together the first night, he probably wouldn't be spending all this time getting to know her. And he was enamored with what he had gotten to know. He could see her passion, but he had also gotten a taste of her wit and her smarts. He wanted more of her—not only under the sheets but also outside the sheets, and that was a rather new prospect for him.

Jeremy put on a short-sleeved white shirt and a pair of khaki slacks. Some socks and his boat moccasins and he was ready to go. He slipped his wallet into his back pocket, clipped his phone onto his belt, dropped his camera into his breast pocket and headed to the State Room to find Safire.

She was already at a table but hadn't gone to the buffet as yet. She was pouring over a sheet of paper in front of her, and as he sat down she started chattering.

"Good morning. I've got it down to Coral World and Bluebeard's Castle, but I think we can have lunch there, so we can save that for later."

He could see her sheer pleasure over the prospects of the day.

"Should I have brought my swimsuit?" he asked.

"Oh. I didn't bring mine, either. I thought we were shopping. Although you can swim at Coral World," she said. "But then we'd have sand in our britches all day."

Jeremy laughed out loud.

"Promise me," he said, "that tomorrow, whatever else we do, we go to either Magen's Bay or Frenchman's Reef."

"You know the island well, don't you?"

"I have college friends from St. Thomas," he said. "I've visited before. But I haven't been to Coral World."

"Perfect. We start at Coral World. We walk the aquar-

ium, pet the fishes in the petting zoo and have our pictures
taken with an iguana."

Jeremy laughed.

"It goes with the picture of me kissing of the dolphin.
Stop laughing." She swatted at him playfully. "Anyway,
then we go to Bluebeard's Castle, and then we can shop
till you drop. Sound good?"

"Sounds wonderful. But let's get some breakfast so we
don't miss the safari."

"I'm too excited. You go ahead."

He took her arm and tugged her to the buffet. "Eat something. For me."

They both had a light breakfast and caught a nine o'clock
safari that would drop them off at Coral World and pick
them up in two hours. He wrapped his arm around her for
the safari ride and linked their fingers once they got to the
aquarium.

He got shots of her petting the starfish and stingray and
other sea creatures in the petting zoo. All he could think
was that he wanted that hand on him. Then she took the
camera from him.

"I'm not petting a stingray," he said. "Do you know why
they call it a stingray?"

She laughed. "I did it. Come on."

"You did, but apparently you don't know why they call
them stingrays." He laughed. Nevertheless, he put his hand
in the water and petted the animal so that she could capture the image.

"Now I just have to get you kissing a dolphin, and we'll
have matching images. Hey, how do I get these from you?"

"I'm sure there's someplace on the ship where we can
burn them onto a CD. We'll check."

They got another tourist to snap a photo of them in front
of the iguanas and then headed down into the circular dome
that led to the ocean floor. The top aquariums were self-

contained, but the bottom wasn't an aquarium at all; the glass opened onto the ocean floor and the animals of the reef.

He loved watching Safire's reaction. He also loved having her hand in his or his arm around her.

She had on orange capris with a light orange sleeveless top that was made out of chiffon with a lining underneath. It billowed out at her hips and made her look ethereal. She had on strappy gold one-inch sandals to go with it. It was all simple, but it made her look simply stunning.

She had also started touching him back—nothing major, but without seeming to think about it, she put her hand on his chest when she pointed out the shark swimming in a huge circle around the aquarium tier. Every time she touched him, it sent a quiver through his body and puffed his ego up just a little bit more. If only she knew what she was doing to him. Later, she grabbed his shoulder and shook it when she realized that what she was seeing was an octopus.

"You just got that?" he teased.

She swatted at him. "Who knew they could curl up like that? Where's the beak?"

"I think we'll have to wait till they feed it."

She checked her watch.

"We better go," she said, "before we miss the safari."

They got something of a tour of the island as they were taxied to Bluebeard's Castle. Then they had a tour of the castle and ate at Room with a View Restaurant. It gave them a chance to sit down and relax and talk for a while.

"So what do you do?" she asked.

"I'm a radiologist. I like it, and it's a good living. What about you?"

"I'm sure it is interesting. And you don't have all the odd hours to contend with, right?"

"I'm on call every other week, but mostly it's nine to

five. It was one of the things that attracted me to the practice. I love work, but I like to have a life as well."

"I'm a teacher. History. And the paper grading and class prep never end." She chuckled. "But I like it."

Jeremy could tell that there was more she was about to say, but she left it at that, so he let it go.

"Where are you from?" he asked.

"North Miami—born and raised. And you?"

"You're from Miami and you've never been on a cruise before?"

"How did you know I haven't been on a cruise?"

"You just seemed a bit awestruck the first day I saw you."

She laughed at that. "I guess so. I was on a cruise with my family when I was little, but I don't really remember it, so I guess this is my first. But what about you? Where are you from?"

"I'm in Miami now," he said, "coming from D.C. I went to Howard University, but I got a good job offer in Miami when I was finished with school, so here I am. I've been in South Miami for a few years. Now I live in Richmond Heights. I like the city, and there's stuff to do, so I don't get bored."

"Do you date a lot?"

"Ouch. Here come the real questions. I date a bit. I like to get out and have fun."

"What does that mean—get out and have fun?" she asked.

"It means that I date, but that I haven't found the right one as yet to make a serious commitment. I'm always open about that." The worried look on her face told him that Safire wasn't too pleased with his answer. "I'm hoping it might be you," he added to temper the news.

"Have you been married before or serious? Do you have any children?"

"You don't hold back, do you?" he said and chuckled. "I don't have children, but I'd like to one day. I have not been married before. I dated a woman in college, but it didn't work out. School took too much of my time, and she didn't understand."

Jeremy noticed that Safire was asking all the questions.

"I don't want to be the only one under the microscope," he said. "What about you? Do you date? Have you been married or serious? Children?"

"No to all of the above. No children. No marriage. No serious relationship, actually. I guess I've spent too much time trying to get my education behind me and then trying to get acclimated to teaching and paying off student loans and dealing with family obligations. I haven't really dated since high school, but that doesn't bother me."

He wanted to ask about her family obligations, but he let it go. There would be time for more details later. For now, it was time for them to get a move on and get some shopping done.

They waited a few minutes for the next safari and took it to downtown Charlotte Amalie. They got off at the waterfront, where there were so many shops that they didn't know what to do.

"Okay," he said. "What are we looking for? I'd like to get something in gold for my mom. Maybe something crystal. That's as far as I know."

"I'm more in the silver range, perhaps some shells or tokens—tight budget."

"That's fine, too."

They held hands as they walked up and down the passages on Main Street, stopping in stores.

He leaned over the counter in the jewelry store, circling her waist where she stood next to him. He kissed her arm, and she laughed and then waved him away. She helped him pick out a rope necklace and matching earrings for his mother, a pair of gold chains for his father and brother, a locket for his grandmother and a watch for his grandfather.

He wished he could get her to pick out something for herself, but he knew that she wouldn't have it. He contented himself with the fact that she was letting him, at least in small ways, be openly affectionate with her.

She got her presents in one of the places that specialized in silver, and then they went to a souvenir shop where he got rum balls and perfume for his coworkers and casual friends, and where she got shells for hers. The rest of their time was spent window shopping, trying tropical-flavored ice creams, and walking Main Street and Back Street before returning to Emancipation Garden to catch a safari.

Along the way, they decided that when they got back to the ship, they would change for dinner, eat and see a movie that night.

"I thought we were going shopping," she said.

"What? We did. We shopped till we dropped. I'm shopped out," he said and then chuckled.

"Look at these teeny little bags we have." Safire held up her little bag of shells and jewelry.

"But these are easier to pack, you see." Jeremy pointed to his little bag of jewelry and perfume.

"Next time, we have to get bigger things. Not more expensive things, just bigger ones. We should look like we just spent four hours doing something."

Both of them laughed.

Back aboard the ship, Jeremy kissed Safire goodbye as if it weref a regular habit between them. He then headed to his room to rest for a little bit, shower and change.

When he got to her stateroom, she was still changing. He lingered at the door, and she was out in a few minutes with a green dress on—a sleeveless one with thin straps. Like the others, it showed off her curves. Like the last one, it was cut close to her body and snug against her breasts.

This time, she had a green shirt over it that was a sheer material. With her strappy one-inch heels and all made up, she looked breathtaking. This woman was growing on him in a very short time.

After dinner in the Captain's Boardroom, they picked a disaster movie and hunkered down in the theater. Jeremy liked the genre, but he liked having Safire curled up on the seat next to him even more, cuddled under his arm in the chill of the cinema.

Still holding her, he slipped his hand up the large sleeve of her cover-up and stroked her forearm, keeping her warm. One of her hands came up to rest on his skin, and to his surprise, she played her fingers over his arm, stirring sensations in his body.

When his forearm caught one of her breasts as he warmed her, he felt the intake of her breath and the spasm in her torso. They had a corner to themselves, so he moved his forearm over her breast again to see if she would respond again. Her chest heaved against his arm, and her fingers tightened on his wrist. He did it again and again until she turned her head into his shoulder and closed her eyes.

When she opened them, she snuggled closer to him and laid her hand on his chest, feeling through his shirt. It was a tentative gesture, but he stopped to see what she would do. She closed her fingers over one of his nipples and created a pressure that sent a hot ripple from his chest down to his swollen groin.

In response, he captured one of her breasts, using his thumb to create a hard crest through the satiny fabric of her dress. Her upper body jerked, and she squirmed in her seat.

When the lights came up, Jeremy was startled. He had spent the entire time watching Safire, not the movie. Under the lights, she smoothed down her dress and adjusted her cover-up, warily checking around to see if anyone had noticed them.

He took a deep breath to collect himself, tugged Safire's hand and drew them both from the theater and toward the elevator.

"Where are we going now?" she asked.

"Home, love."

He felt the questions rise in her, but she remained silent and let herself be drawn along his path.

As the door to his stateroom closed, Jeremy pulled Safire into his arms and a passionate kiss, pressing every inch of her against his body, which had been teased for too long. She responded to his touch, but she was quiet. He broke the kiss to put on one of the dimmer lights next to the bed.

When he turned back, he found Safire still at the door, her arms clasped protectively in front of her chest, one of her ankles teetering nervously upon the heel of her shoe. Now that they were alone, her hesitance was back. He could see in her a shyness that made her seem vulnerable and plucked at his heart.

He didn't want to frighten her away, and he was more than willing to go at her pace, but God, he wanted her so badly that he was going to have a hard time if she didn't want him back tonight. One thing was clear. The desire between them was unmistakable. The only question was whether or not she was ready to give in to those feelings.

He crossed back to her and took her in his arms again, pressing her lightly against the door. He held her body flush with his, knowing she could feel his sex wedged against her center. He pressed himself into her and kissed her until her hips tilted forward, seeking the feel of him. He deepened his kiss until her hips rocked against his, riding her almost imperceptibly along his manhood. He thrust his tongue deep into her mouth until it elicited a choked whimper that set his pulse on fire.

How he wanted her.

When he tore his mouth from hers, she held him tightly

around his shoulders, as if she didn't want him to see her. Jeremy dipped his head to her neck, kissing the tender flesh. He opened her cover-up and bent down to press his lips over one of her breasts though her dress. Her body twisted, and her arms tightened about his head.

Slipping from her embrace, he lowered himself onto his knees in front of her, nudging through her dress at the center of her womanhood. He wanted to take his time, but the beauty of this woman was urging him onward. He heard her breath catch as he raised the hem of her dress and brought his mouth to her panties, kneading her sex through the slick shield of thin cotton. She was so wet, so ready, that it was all he could do to keep his knees on the ground.

His palms on her hips pinned her to the back of the door, but her hips swirled against them. She was rather quiet, but he could tell that she loved his mouth upon her. Her breathing, the way her hands tightened around his head, and the taut thrust of her groin told him that.

He hooked his thumbs in the material at her hips. He might be pushing it, but he couldn't help it. He wanted her. Her hands flew to his wrists as he began to pull down the intruding underwear.

He stopped, but her panties were already clear of her sex. He kissed her intimately, parted her slick path with his tongue and sucked her into his mouth. Her body jerked against the door, and she shuddered, gripping his wrists. Safire was making his body blaze.

Still, she hadn't let go. His tongue and lips toyed over her; his mouth drank in her honeyed liquor; his nose took in her floral scent. Still, she was choking back her murmurs and biting off moans.

When he moved one of his hands up to her breast, her hips rocked her core onto his mouth. She quivered, clipped short a wail and gripped his shoulders. His fingers spread over both of her breasts, tweaking and groping the hard nipples, and his mouth continued to graze her inflamed sex. He was ready, as ready as she was.

Her hips went taut.

Just as she cried out, she cut off the sound, and it fell to a low whimper.

Jeremy looked up at Safire, smiling. She was biting her lower lip. Her eyes were closed, and she was trying to catch her breath. He rubbed the outsides of her thighs to comfort her.

When she opened her eyes, however, her hands sprang across her chest. An expression of shock came onto her face.

She fumbled awkwardly to raise her panties, toppling him backward in front of her. Before he could right himself or say a word, she had slipped through the cabin door behind her and escaped down the hallway. When he got to the door, there was no sign of her, not even the imprint of her shoes on the carpet was left.

Chapter 5

Angelina didn't take Jeremy's calls that night. She got back to her stateroom and began pacing in a furious circle, trying to take in what had happened and how things had gotten out of her hands so quickly.

Sensations still coursed through her body. It still throbbed from his touch, his mouth. She poured herself a glass of lukewarm water from her melted ice bucket to try to calm down, but she couldn't.

His touches set her body humming, and he'd been touching her all day long. She had wanted to be with him, had wanted to let herself go, but in the end, she'd been appalled by what she'd done, gyrating before him like a cat in heat. She didn't know if she could even face him again.

What's more, she'd then run away without giving him... anything. That made it even worse. Why couldn't she simply enjoy the moment? What would she do if she had to look him in the eyes again?

The pacing wasn't helping. Unable to figure any of it out, she checked in at home to make sure that all was well, changed out of Safire's green dress, and got under the covers for the night. She had a fitful sleep, dreaming of warm brown eyes.

In the morning her head was clearer, but she still didn't know if she could face him again. She knew when the phone rang that it could only be him. She answered it not knowing what she would say.

"Good morning, beautiful," he said, as if nothing had happened last night.

"Hello."

His tone was casual. "I wanted to take you to breakfast. Are you fully up yet?"

"About last night...I'm sorry. It—" She didn't know what else to say.

"I guess things were moving a little quickly."

"Yes."

"It was still beautiful to me."

His low voice in her ear sent goose bumps down her neck and heated her center.

"I was...silly."

"You were beautiful," he said.

She was quiet. Jeremy's words put her a bit at ease, but the image in her mind of last night mortified her.

He seemed unfazed. "I would love to do that again— and more. But we can go at your pace."

She heard sincerity in his voice and decided to believe him.

"So, what now?" she asked.

"I'm thinking breakfast. Then maybe some swimming at Magen's Bay."

She smiled, but could she face him? Before her mind had decided, she heard herself saying yes.

"I'll put on my swimsuit and grab a towel. Where should we meet?"

"I'll be there by the time you pack your bag."

"Okay."

When she stepped into the hall, he was just turning the corner, a bag over his arm, a smile on his face and a long-stemmed rose in his hand. But she still had to actually face him after last night. She swallowed, not knowing what to expect, but he simply kissed her cheek, wrapped her in a brief hug and took her tote bag.

She could tell that she must be blushing, but he didn't seem to notice. She was only able to release the tension in her shoulders once they were out among people, back to getting to know one another. After breakfast they caught a safari to Magen's Bay.

The countryside was beautiful, and nearing the beach, trees arched down over the roadway. They bought drinks and then found a spot on the smooth, white sand. While Jeremy was stripping off his shorts and T-shirt, she spread her towel out on the sand, found her sunglasses, and lay down.

"Aren't you going to take things off?" he asked.

Angelina took her shorts off and lay back down. Jeremy had gotten out his lotion.

"I can't get your back with your shirt on."

Angelina sat up and hugged her legs.

"Is something wrong?"

"Well, I forgot to bring my bathing suit. This one is borrowed and not quite to my…specifications."

"We're on St. Thomas. No one cares what your bathing suit looks like. Come. Let me give you a massage," he suggested.

Reluctantly, she pulled her T-shirt over her head and balled it up next to her. She was wearing Safire's bikini, the kind of thing she never wore. And though the sisters were similar in stature, Angelina was slightly better endowed in the front and the rear. She could feel the little straps cutting into her rump, and her breasts were almost pouring from the tiny little triangles in front—or at least she felt as if they were.

Jeremy's jaw dropped. His eyes caressed her desirously.

"You look great in that," he said. "It fits you like a glove."

Angelina relaxed a bit, seeing the admiration in his eyes. After he got the lotion on her, he lifted her up.

"What are you doing?"

He was heading for the surf. He got her into waist-high

water and then lifted her to throw her in, but she clung to his neck, and only her legs dropped. Both of them were laughing.

"Hey," she said after gaining her footing. "The water is warm. Let's go in."

She took off under the water, and he dove in to follow. They swam out a bit, then swam the length of the rounded, heart-shaped shore and came back.

"You're a real swimmer," he said as they gained their footing near the shoreline.

"I love the water. And this is so blue. Stand up and look down at your feet. You can see the little fish swimming around them."

"Yeah, you can."

They were neck deep in crystal-blue water. He lifted her in the water and spun her around, taking her into his arms to kiss her. She wrapped her arms around his neck, laughing, until the kiss became more serious. She could feel him beginning to swell against her.

He let her down, a wistful look in his eyes, and they started to swim again, this time to the other end of Magen's Bay. After swimming and playing in the water for almost two hours, they padded back up to their towels.

"You're not from Florida," she said. "How did you learn to swim so well?"

"Actually, I was raised in Texas. My parents are still there. I went to Howard University, and as an undergraduate, you had to take swimming. I swam at the YMCA as a kid, but I got a C in swimming."

She laughed. He did, too.

"That's not funny. It brought my grade point average down." That made her laugh harder. "I was then determined to master the art."

"You had to take swimming?"

"At Howard, you still have to take swimming in Arts and Sciences."

"If I wasn't from North Miami, it might have brought my average down as well. But you're not a nerd."

Jeremy laughed. "Thank you, I guess. I played a bit in high school, though. I knew if I wanted to go on, I had to do well, so I was pretty determined in college. What about you?"

"I wanted the A. I got a B in chemistry lab and freaked out. I guess that's one of the reasons I'm not a doctor now. Book stuff I could do. Practical application with beakers and Bunsen burners and goggles—no."

They both laughed.

"Did you ever actually aspire to medical school?" he asked.

"No, I was always more arts than sciences."

"I guess I was always more sciences than arts. I had to work in English, and I mean *work*."

They both laughed again. Angelina wanted to tell him about her writing, but something stopped her. It was personal, as personal as sex, and as usual, she held back. After last night, maybe she didn't need to. But the moment had passed.

After drying off in the sun, they caught the safari back to the ship. They had lunch, but after that, reason got the better of her. She hadn't gotten much work done yet, so she begged off. He had dinner plans with his boys, so they decided to meet afterward. She could pick the activity.

She showered, rinsed out her sister's swimsuit and spent the afternoon at the table in her room working on the syllabus for one of her classes and making notes for her paper on World War II political activism by Black women in Harlem.

Around six o'clock, she grabbed a sandwich and then camped out on the balcony with the Patterman book. After several chapters, though, she brought her laptop out to work on her creative writing.

That's what she was doing when Jeremy called at a quarter of eight.

"Are you ready?" he asked.

"Dress comfortably, and meet me at the elevator on my side on the ninth deck."

"What are we doing?"

"You'll see."

She already had on her jeans and a loose top, so she pulled on her sneakers, grabbed her room key, and headed out. She had picked the perfect activity for them.

He stepped off the elevator in casual slacks and a shirt.

"What are we doing?" he asked, seeing her mischievous grin.

"Skating."

"Are you kidding?"

"No. They have an inline skating rink."

"Okay, but I don't actually know how to Rollerblade."

"Neither do I."

They both laughed. They rented skates and had a hilarious time learning how to use them. At first, they held on to each other for support but only managed to topple each other over in the effort, giggling like kids. More than once Angelina found herself cushioned by Jeremy's body—horizontal on the floor. And to her dismay, getting up in skates was much harder than falling down.

Once they managed to stay upright and get themselves parallel to one another, they locked hands and took slow, tentative glides—a foot or two to begin. In an hour or so, they were becoming rather proficient.

"I wonder," Angelina said, "if they'd let us skate through one of the gardens."

"We can stand," Jeremy said, considering it. "But we'd still be a public menace."

They both laughed.

"Okay, then that has to be next," she said. "That or window shopping."

"I think the stores are closed now."

"That's why it's just window shopping."

They laughed again.

Next they headed to the Admiral's Arbor, one of the gardens. Both were surprised by how big it was. They held hands and wandered between the flowerbeds and hedge work. Then they found a bench with an ocean view and rested for a bit, their legs sore from skating.

He put an arm around her and held her hip. She pulled her legs up underneath her and leaned back under the stars.

"Would you rather be dancing or doing something?" she asked.

"No, my legs could stand the break."

"Mine too," she admitted and chuckled.

He followed her gaze up toward the night sky. "And it's beautiful out here at night."

"Yes."

"And you're cute in jeans and sneakers."

When he kissed her, Angelina knew she had to make up her mind. She would either take Safire's advice or she needed to put the brakes on right then, and if he ran away, so be it. She put her hand up to his chest. He sat up and looked at her, drawing his free hand onto her thigh and squeezing it gently.

"We don't have to do anything, Safire. I just want to be here with you."

His statement made up her mind. She leaned toward him and kissed his lips. She took a breath and then kissed him again, opening her mouth to him and feeling his tongue slip inside and fill her with heat.

"I know," she said when they pulled apart.

He didn't let her retreat for long. His brought his face

to hers and took her mouth again, moving his hand up to touch her breast through her blouse. He had no idea how that turned her on.

Or maybe he did. When his fingers made her nipples constrict against her bra and brought a low murmur from her throat, he smiled against her lips.

She blushed and swatted at him, pulling back and pushing him away as he laughed.

"Don't be mad," he said. "I love how responsive your body is to me. You have the same effect on me."

"What do we do now?"

"You tell me, my love."

She toyed with the fingers intertwined with hers and then sighed. Jeremy's warm brown eyes seemed to beckon to her up close, and his thick, soft lips seemed to wait for her taste. The smooth brown skin over his rigid cheekbones seemed ready for her touch, and his angular brow seemed to crinkle in anticipation of what she would say. The cultured beauty of this man was waiting to be claimed. Her heart was skipping, and her palms were starting to sweat.

"Come home with me," she said.

"Are you sure?" he asked.

"No. Yes. I don't know."

He took her hand and pulled her up from the bench.

"You think about it on the way."

The walk to her room took almost twenty minutes, and the closer they got, the more nervous Angelina felt. When Jeremy paused at her door to look into her face, she had to take a deep breath. She pressed her palm to the pit of her stomach to try to calm the butterflies. He noticed.

"We don't have to."

"I know."

She steadied her hand to use her keycard, let them in the door and turned on the light. For a moment, she stood there, looking at the room as if it weren't hers, checking to make sure she hadn't left undies thrown around or books strewn over the place.

He didn't let her stand there long. He drew her into the room and into his arms. His lips covered her mouth, and his hands covered her breasts, and soon she didn't remember the room anymore. She couldn't think of anything but the feelings coursing through her body.

When they stopped for a breath, she let her head rest against his cheek. Since her lips were already poised to do so, she kissed his neck. In response, he groaned softly and shook his head.

"I told you that you do the same thing to me," he said.

He rubbed the outside of her thighs and then put a hand between them to knead her body through the thick weave of her jeans. She felt her hips tilt forward against his palm. Her body wanted that touch.

Startling her, he turned her around and pulled her back against his chest. He caught her breast beneath his palm and continued the undulating massage through her jeans. She felt heat flowing into her center and moisture flowing to meet his need.

He undid her jeans and allowed her to step out of them, along with her sneakers, and he pulled her blouse over her head.

Then he sat on the bed and looked at her body. Her hands had come up automatically, and he pulled them toward him, wrapping them around his neck as he moved his mouth over her bra, capturing one of her breasts. He released the fastener and pulled her breast into his mouth. Fire licked through her chest.

When his fingers found her throbbing sex through her moistened panties, she sucked in her breath and then bit off the moan that wanted to pour through her throat.

He stood and pulled her against his body, settling her against his rigid manhood. She moaned softly and her hips pressed forward. She wanted to feel more. He cupped her rear and ground her against him until she moaned again, against her own will, until she thrust against his swollen center, against her own will.

He kissed her as he motioned her onto the bed, but she drew him with her, using his body to cover her near nakedness. He took her breast into his mouth and starting gently rubbing her womanhood through her thin gauze. His fingers found her center, and she whimpered in delicious agony.

With his fingers playing over her sex and his tongue licking the hard peak of her nipple, Angelina couldn't think, couldn't swallow, couldn't breathe. She thrust with need against his hand. She couldn't believe what she was doing, but she couldn't stop. Her hips jerked, bringing her against his palm and sending her to the edge.

When his mouth left her breast, she winced, and without thinking, she lowered her hands from his head to clasp her own needy mounds. His tongue worked its way through her fingers, flicking at a taut crown. She gyrated against his fingers and cried out as lightning flashed through her sex and she fell over the brink.

Angelina opened her eyes to find Jeremy looking at her. She was disconcerted by what she had just done, flailing about in front of him. She couldn't bear the easy look on his face or the soft grin on his lips. She didn't want him to see her.

She started to jump from the bed, but his arm came around her waist. He literally lifted her back down, stroking her hair and kissing her forehead.

"Don't go, Safire. That was…beautiful. I loved that. Don't let it be over."

"I—I—"

"Didn't you like it?"

He touched his forehead to hers and kissed her nose.

"Yes."

"Then we're not finished yet."

He wrapped his arms around her and drew her close against his chest.

"Can we make love?"

She clung to his arms, her embarrassment subsiding.

"Please say yes."

Angelina heard the hunger in Jeremy's entreaty and knew what it meant to be the object of human longing. She saw the rapture in his eyes and knew without hesitation that she wanted to fulfill that need. She nodded.

Jeremy got up and took off his clothes. His firm shoulders and sculpted arms, his broad chest and tapered flank, his full thighs and thick, leaping sex—all of his masculine beauty, fully nude, came into view under Angelina's open gaze. He pulled his wallet out of his slacks and took out a condom, and when he had sheathed himself, he joined her on the bed again.

He pulled off her panties and touched her, lighting her on fire all over again. Angelina thought that he would climb on top of her, but instead, he turned her away, letting her breasts fall into his palm and spreading her thighs with his own so that he could feel her slippery wetness. His fingers slid over her sex, filling her with desire.

He moved himself into place, and she couldn't help murmuring.

"Are you ready, baby?"

She nodded again.

"Safire," he called.

She turned back to see his face.

"Yes?"

"Are you sure you want this?"

"Yes, Jeremy."

He kissed her and then slowly thrust inside of her. He

paused and sucked in his breath and groaned. Then he moved farther inside.

With one hand cupping her breasts and the other teasing her swollen precipice, he began to thrust inside of her. Angelina couldn't help moaning quietly as his manhood filled her and rocked inside her, filling her with yearning and driving her toward the brink.

His long, slow thrusts made her wince, made her center cling to his, made her toss on the bedspread, pressing back against him. His short, fast plunges massaged her pleasure points, making her writhe and groan. His lips at her back made her shiver with anticipation, and his fingers at her breasts and sex made her ready to explode. All combined, his touches drove her body to its limit of indulgence. She heard his moan and felt his body tense, and she cried out as he pushed her over that edge.

Chapter 6

Jeremy had pulled the cover over them, and they had slept with her spooned in his arms. Now he woke up remembering how incredibly tight Safire had been when he moved inside of her, how her womanhood had clung to his stiffness, how the waves of her climax had driven him to his own. He could tell that she had not been with anyone in some time.

But where was she? The room was empty. His clothes were piled neatly in one of her chairs. He grabbed his shorts and his pants, pulled them on and went toward the bathroom, calling her name.

The glass door to the balcony slid open, and she came in with a book in her hand. He moved toward her and kissed her.

He checked his watch. "It's after nine."

"You seemed so peaceful asleep."

"With you in my arms, I slept like a baby."

She flushed a little, and he kissed her cheek again. He loved the shyness in her almost as much as he loved it when she lost control.

"We've docked at Puerto Rico," she said. "I have a ticket for a tour. Care to come with me?"

"I'd love to. Can I get a ticket now?"

"Let's call and check."

"Then a late lunch?" he asked.

She went to him and patted his tummy. "Hungry?"

He chuckled.

"Starved." He lunged for her, lifted her and carried her to the bed. "But not for what you think."

She scampered from his clutches, laughing.

"It's getting late. We have to see about another ticket."

He cornered her at the headboard and kissed her.

"Okay, but tonight is another story."

She squealed when he pulled her down the length of the bed by her ankles and tickled her, laughing all the while. She squirmed out of his grasp and onto her feet, holding up her palms to him.

"Okay," he conceded.

"You have to dress, anyway. I showered this morning, so all I have to do is change."

He glanced over her. "You look fine."

"But the tour includes one of the churches, and I want to see inside."

"Okay. I'll wear something presentable."

"Bring your camera," she added. "The rainforest is supposed to be beautiful."

"It is."

He winked at her, kissed her nose and left her. He strode through the hall elated, stopping to leap toward one of the recessed lights as if he was dunking a basketball into a hoop. He had that much energy. And it wasn't all from how good it felt to make love to her finally. Playing with Safire outside of the sheets was as awesome as it had been under the covers—and that was…fantastic.

Back in his room, he called Alistair, who was with Rudy at one of the pools, and let him know that he'd be gone for the day.

"No surprise there. You getting any?"

"M-Y-O-B, sweetie. Mind your own business."

"Whoo-hoo," Alistair said. "I know what that means."

He heard Alistair and Rudy high five each other.

"Stop it. We're not five years old anymore."

"We certainly are not," Alistair said, being saucy.

"See you guys later."

Jeremy showered and changed before calling Safire. There was space available on the tour bus, but they had to skip breakfast. They were both okay with that.

The tour started with the El Yunque rainforest. Even on the way up, the bus stopped so that they could see natural waterfalls off the side of the road. Near the top, they got out and walked up a path to the interior.

Along the way, their guide pointed out the flora and fauna. They stopped at another waterfall, and guests had a chance to wade in the water. Jeremy wasn't inclined, but he watched as Safire took off her shoes, tied her skirt between her legs and waded in. The sight of her that way was erotic, and when she realized he was photographing her, she started to laugh and then splashed him.

After she had had some fun, she came over to him. He had found a comfortable rock and was relaxing. She spread one of his legs and sat on the other. She wrapped her arms around his neck and kissed him and then laughed.

"Am I too heavy?"

He bounced her on his knee a couple of times in answer.

"Show off," she said and swatted him. She pulled his head to her chest and squeezed him. Then she kissed his forehead and let him go.

He loved that she was getting comfortable being affectionate with him. Of course, they were in public, and nothing could come of it, but he liked it anyway. Almost as good, she didn't seem to notice it when he touched her, or at least she didn't seem self-conscious about it anymore. Her body still reacted to him, though, and he still liked to make it do just that. And she was laughing a lot today. He liked that, too.

They hiked back to the bus and headed for Old San Juan. The walking tour started at La Casita and then went through the Paseo La Princesa promenade, a long walk along the city's outer wall with gardens and street vendors. They got a picture in front of its large bronze sculpture and then another at the San Juan Gate.

Safire spent most of her time looking at the sights, but he was spending most of his time looking at Safire. Everything about her was growing on him. The heat she kept in his loins was turning into the least of his distractions. She had a glow about her. She also has a sense of humor. She especially loved the history of things and asked questions about El Morro, one of the forts.

She loved the San Juan Cathedral, and when the tour was over and they had some time to wander the city, they went back for more pictures. They found a restaurant farther up the street—Cristo Street—and then visited some of the nearby craft shops and art galleries.

She seemed to love the arts and crafts. He knew that she didn't have a lot of money to spend, but she kept thinking about an art piece at one of the galleries, as if weighing the cost against the penny-pinching she would have to do later on, when she had to make up for it. It was a painting of an old Puerto Rican couple with a basket of flowers.

As she stared at it, he wrapped his arms around her and kissed her neck, wondering why she liked it so much.

"You like this one?"

"Yes, I do."

But she didn't say more. In the end, she got a small wooden statue and some postcards of the artwork as keepsakes, and they both picked up business cards from the shop. He wrapped his arm around her, and she put her arm around him, and they continued on.

On the bus, she rested her head on his shoulder and put her hand in his. He couldn't help inhaling the aroma of her hair and running his fingers through it, appreciating their closeness. Yes, this woman was beginning to grow on him.

And even with the slight touch of their fingers together, he could feel the desire rising between them.

Underneath his desire, Jeremy felt a growing tenderness for this woman— her inquisitiveness, her wit, her presence, her ways. He was proud to have her at his side, to be the one whose fingers linked with hers. The allure of her body had been magnified for him by the beauty of her spirit, and together, these were tugging at all of his strings. The more taken he was with her charm, the more heated his desire became. It was a powerful cycle—yearning and tenderness, more yearning and more tenderness—and Jeremy loved being trapped in its rotation.

Back on the ship, they decided to get some swimming in before dinner.

"Would you like to meet a couple of my friends?" he asked.

"I guess so, if you think they'd like to meet me."

He called Alistair. He and Rudy were still at one of the pools and had been joined by Myron and Verniece.

He and Safire changed into swimsuits and met up again to go to the pool.

"You know Myron and Verniece," he said. "This is Alistair, my oldest friend, and Rudy, my friend since college. This is Safire."

"Pleased to meet you."

Alistair was tall and lanky, but well toned from his constant occupation of the gym. He had an open face and a boyish grin. That grin now took on a sly twist as he took Safire's arm and brought her to the lounge chairs.

"Now let's see who's been occupying all of Jeremy's time."

Jeremy was a little worried; his best friend was gay and fairly judgmental. Likewise, he wasn't sure what Safire's response would be, if she was socially conservative, but she simply smiled and settled in next to him.

"And let me get all the dirt about this one here, who's been monopolizing my time so that none of my work is getting done," Safire said.

Jeremy went to get drinks for Safire and himself, and he came back to find the two into their conversation and laughing. He returned to Rudy at the bar but kept an eye on them, wondering what they were talking about.

"Okay, you have to set me up with Michelle," Rudy was saying.

Michelle was one of Jeremy's best friends. He didn't know if Rudy would be a good match for her.

"What about the one-night stand you just had?"

Rudy had made a connection their second night on the ship.

"It was just that—a one-night stand."

Jeremy tore his eyes from Safire and Alistair and looked back at Rudy. His friend was on the shorter side and a bit round—plump, Rudy would say—but with a sociable disposition. Michelle was a stunner and fairly particular—not so much about looks but about overall comportment. Rudy didn't always act his age and could be a bit adolescent at times. He might not even be earnest about this. Jeremy faced him, square and sober.

"Are you serious about Michelle?"

"I know I could be."

This wasn't quite the answer Jeremy would have wanted, but it was honest, so he nodded.

"I'll see what I can do."

They touched cups as if they were wineglasses, and then Jeremy got up to go see what his friend and his girl were up to.

When he got near, he heard a snippet of their conversation.

"…when he was three, so when he was five, he peed in a cup of Kool-Aid to see if it would turn green."

Safire was laughing heartily, and Alistair was chatting away.

"Wait. What color was the Kool-Aid?"

"Red."

They both cracked up.

"Aw," Safire said. "If it was blue, it might have worked."

He had no intention of letting his friend continue.

"How on earth did you get onto this subject?" Jeremy held his hand out for Safire.

"Wait, wait. We're only up to five."

He got hold of Safire's hand and started to tug her upward.

"We were having quite a good time, thank you," Alistair said.

"Well, you'll have to finish later."

"We do," Safire said. "Five. Don't forget."

Jeremy scowled at his friend and tugged at Safire's clothes. She was still giggling as she removed her T-shirt and shorts. He wrapped his arms around her and started edging her toward the pool. "I'll get you later," he called back to Alistair.

For now, as revenge, he lifted up Safire, who was still chuckling, and tossed her into the pool.

They swam and played for about an hour, and whatever initial shyness she might have had around his friends disappeared with their play.

At about eight, the group started to gather for dinner. They went to one of the casual restaurants and ordered burgers. Over dinner, Safire and Alistair got them all talking about Jeremy's bloopers and laughing. Alistair added ones from his childhood—like the time he ripped the back seat of his pants trying to learn how to ride a bicycle without training wheels.

Both Myron and Rudy added ones from his college days. Rudy, for example, blabbed about the first time he'd tried on a condom. He pulled it the wrong way, and it snapped back against his skin. He had to put ice on his nether region and had a welt that lasted for over a week. Why had he ever told Rudy such a thing?

Jeremy scowled at his friends, but he didn't really mind being the butt of their stories given the smile it put on Safire's face. And he loved the sound of her laughter.

After dinner, the group was planning to meet again for a movie.

"Oh, I can't," Safire said. "I have to do a bit of work."

"I'll see you guys tomorrow," Jeremy said.

Alistair gave him wink as he took Safire's hand and headed toward the elevator.

"My place first," Jeremy said.

"Your place?"

"I'm still hungry," he said, bending down to kiss her.

"I do have a few things to do."

"I'll try to get you home before it's too late."

They were both still damp, but once inside his stateroom, Jeremy dispensed with the idea of them showering together and took Safire into his arms. She met his kiss and brought her arms up to his shoulders.

He stepped back. "Let me get you out of these wet things."

She smiled, only the slightest hesitation in her stance. Then she let him pull the T-shirt over her head and the shorts from her hips, untying her bikini straps as he went along. She shivered, and he drew her to the bed, lifting the covers for her to climb in.

He pulled a condom from his drawer, shrugged off his clothes, and crawled in next to her.

At first, he just held her in his arms, liking the feel of her soft skin against his rough flesh, the feel of her peaked breasts against his hard chest, the feel of her silky legs against his tense thighs.

He was already turned on, but he knew he wanted to take his time with her. He wanted this to be right. He kissed her and used his tongue to spell out his passion. One of his arms was wrapped under her body, and he ran his fingers along her shoulder. The way her body tensed told him when he reached a sensitive spot. His other hand was free, and he caressed her breasts, feeling her torso begin to twitch.

Every signal from her body sent electricity coursing through his manhood. He was very ready, but he wanted her to be ready, too. Her nipples were hard under the spell of his fingertips, but he wanted more. He wanted to touch her. He moved downward, touching his lips to her chest.

When his mouth covered her breast, her hips glided against him, and she murmured. Her body was lighting his on fire. He pulled her leg over his hip and moved his hand between them. She moaned and twisted as he neared her sex, and when he found it, she moaned again and shivered.

"Oh, touch me. Please touch me," she whispered.

Her request, her voice, the thickness of its desire, made his manhood leap. He began to massage her, and she began to rock against his hand. When his fingers slipped inside her swollen valley, he found her slick with moisture, and how wet she was, how ready she was, made his body thicken and made him groan.

He stopped and felt along the bed for the condom, and when he'd put it on, he raised himself over her, dragging his chest along her breasts. She hummed with pleasure. He brought himself to her entry and paused a moment to calm down, wanting to take his time.

He felt her hips rotating beneath him. She was rubbing herself along his member, making him rigid, making him needy with every movement. He loved how she was taking pleasure from him, but he knew he couldn't keep still for very long.

He claimed her mouth as he plunged inside her body, swallowing her moan.

He loved when she moaned. And he loved that she was letting herself do so freely.

As he rocked inside of her, she tilted her hips to ride her womanhood along his lower abdomen and her breasts along his chest. She winced and thrust harder upon him.

"Jeremy," she called out.

"Yes, anything."

"Jeremy, don't stop."

She was driving him toward climax.

"I won't, Safire."

Her body tensed and started jerking onto his in short jabs. She cried out, and as she did he felt the waves of her climax moving along his manhood. She cried out as her sex clamped onto his, riding him. She called his name as she pressed taut against him, taking in the wave of her pleasure and pushing him over the edge.

He turned them on the bed to wrap her in his arms. He was amazed by this woman.

Chapter 7

Angelina woke up wrapped in Jeremy's arms, weak from the pleasures of the previous night. She looked at her watch and closed her eyes again. They only had two more full days together—today and tomorrow. What would happen then?

She tried to move from his arms without disturbing him, but as she pulled away from him, he shifted closer, holding her tighter. She tried again, and the same thing happened. On the third try, low, grumbling laughter came from deep in his chest.

"Are you trying to get away?" he asked.

"Yes, I am. And you're wide awake."

"It's early, and I like holding you."

"Well, I have a day."

He opened his eyes, "Are you going ashore?"

"We could later, but I have a spa appointment this morning."

"I see. And you were trying to sneak away."

He chuckled, grabbing her firmly by the hips and pulling her against the length of his body. He was warm and hard, and starting to swell. She raised herself up on her elbow and kissed his shoulder. He opened his eyes again to look at her.

"I was trying not to wake you before I got my clothes on and did something with my hair."

He had taken the band from her ponytail the night before. Now he took her mane in his fist and pulled her down toward him. He kissed her neck.

"Your hair is beautiful loose. You look amazing."

She didn't buy it but was grateful that he said so.

"Since you're up," she said, "how about breakfast? Or do you want to get some more sleep?"

"No, I'm fine for sleep. You want to shower together?"

"Okay, but at my place." But then, she wasn't sure she wanted him to be able to examine her naked body under glaring white lights. "Or I can just head home and come back in a little bit. Why don't I do that?"

He gathered that she was chickening out and chuckled again, toppling her onto her back and pulling the covers down her body.

"Hey, no fair."

She slid down the bed to stay under the covers, and he laughed. She finally got hold of the bedspread and wrapped it around her body as she stood.

"You don't have anything to feel shy about. You're beautiful."

Jeremy patted the bed for her to come back, but the devilish glint in his eyes warned Angelina away.

"No, I'm going home to get dressed before you start anything."

She slipped on her shorts and T-shirt and balled up Safire's bikini. She picked up her pool bag and glanced over her shoulder.

"I'll call you in a little while, when I'm ready."

"I'll be there before you're done."

She left him on the bed, half covered and looking sexy as all get-out.

Angelina made it to her stateroom in a disheveled state and started setting things in order. It didn't take her long to rinse out the swimsuit, shower, change, and pick up odds and ends from around the room. She was actually ready when Jeremy knocked.

During breakfast, they made plans for the day. Then he walked her to the spa and left her with a kiss.

She'd never had a spa treatment before. Safire had pre-ordered the basic package, no doubt because of the cost of everything else. She was to have a whirlpool spa and a massage, followed by her face, hair, feet and nails.

In the whirlpool, she tried to figure out what to do about all of the work she wasn't getting done and what to do with their last two days. She knew that she wouldn't get much finished, so the issue was damage control—figuring out what had to be completed immediately when she got home, what could be done later.

What if she was still seeing Jeremy when she got back? She didn't know how to calculate that into the equation of things or even if it would be an issue. Secretly, she hoped it would be.

She had never had a massage before. At first it was scary being naked, but after she was put at ease, it was wonderful. She wished they were Jeremy's hands on her, though, and the thought of him sent a shiver up her spine.

Though it had been such a short time, she had gotten used to having him around, used to planning her days with him, used to having him underfoot as she tramped about. She was getting attached, and with their time together coming to an end, she didn't know what to do about that except to wait and see.

When she was done at the spa, she felt like a queen, all done up. She decided to get dressed up to match her new hair and nails and face. She also knew she was doing it to get a reaction out of Jeremy, but she didn't care.

A couple of her own conservative skirts were still clean. She had one more of her sister's dresses left, but it was the most revealing of them all. It was a one-shoulder, sleeveless dress in a beautiful orange brocade material, and it barely passed the tops of her thighs. She also had a sheer burnt-sienna cover-up that she could put with it. They didn't quite match, but she decided to try them on.

The sheer shirt was longer than the dress itself, so she added a belt. It wasn't bad with the cover-up, and she added her strappy gold sandals to show off her pedicure. It made her feel sexy. There must be a bit of Safire in her, after all.

She and Jeremy had decided to skip the tour of Grand Turk and hang out on the ship. When she was done dressing, she called to check in at home. Then she called Jeremy, who was ready to meet her, and they decided on a place.

When she approached him in the Butterfly Lounge, he stood up, and his mouth gaped.

"You look gorgeous."

She smiled and kissed him, grateful for his reaction.

"Thank you. I've been pampered like a princess."

"You look like one."

"You look good, too."

And he did. He had on a casual suit and a pinstripe shirt. The blazer showed off his wide shoulders, and the slacks could barely contain his dense thighs and full rear. His features were clean and chiseled, set off by those warm brown eyes. He smiled at her compliment and nodded.

"Well, where are we off to?" he asked.

"Let's have a snack first. I'm a little hungry. What do they have here?"

They split a sandwich and shared a virgin strawberry daiquiri. Then he took her hand and they strolled about the decks for a while. After that they hit the shopping district. There were so many shops that they didn't know which ones to go into. They stopped in the candy store, several clothing stores, the toy store, the book store and a variety of other places along the strip.

She loved the way he put his arm around her, and she

loved when he put his hand on her back or held her hand as they went along. She was growing to love his touch. In fact, her feelings for him were becoming stronger all the time. In one of the clothing stores, it occurred to her that she could tell him her real name now. They had shared just about everything else.

"Jeremy?"

"Yes, love."

"My name—"

"What can I do for you today?" a sales clerk interrupted them.

"We were just looking," Jeremy replied, "but do you have any polo shirts?"

"Oh, yes. Come this way."

Jeremy put a hand on her back, letting her go in front of him.

"You were saying? Your name?"

With other people about, Angelina didn't feel comfortable pursuing the confession. She could still get in a great deal of trouble—the kind she didn't want to think about.

She kissed him on the cheek and smiled at him.

"It can wait until we get home. Let's look for your shirts."

They didn't do much actual shopping, but she got some more postcards and a handheld game, and he got a T-shirt, some polo shirts that she helped him to pick out and a couple of mystery books.

They went to an early concert—a large cast of actors doing Broadway classics—and then they went to a formal dining room because he said he wanted to show her off while she was all done up. She laughed at the suggestion and twirled around so that he could see her. Then she laughed again—at herself—for being so bold. She could only be this way with Jeremy.

The tables in the Pearls of the Sea Restaurant seated ten, so they ordered surf-and-turf and spent dinner chatting with the other guests about the cruise, politics and their time at sea.

At her door, she put her arms around Jeremy's neck, pressed her body to his and kissed him.

"If you keep doing that," he said, "we'll have to change our plans for the evening."

She stepped back, smiling. "Are you sure you want to do this? You could be hanging out with your friends."

He held up his shopping bags. "Nope, I'm ready."

Since she needed to get some work done, they had decided to get in some reading. He pulled out one of his new mystery books, and she opened the textbook for one of her classes to do a reading schedule. They bunked out on the balcony in lounge chairs and settled down to their tasks.

Angelina was worried about trying to get work done with Jeremy around. He was on vacation, after all. But she would rather be distracted by his presence than not have it. It actually worked for a while.

After a couple of hours, however, she was the one who did the distracting.

She got up to get another book and turn on the light, but before doing either of those things, she was drawn to his chair.

He was a quarter of the way through his novel, but the light was beginning to dim. She sat on the edge of his lounge chair, facing him, and took the book from his hands, laying it open on the table next to the chair.

"Do you mind?" she asked.

"No."

He had a gleam in his eye that let her know he wanted whatever came next.

She leaned forward and pressed her lips to his, savoring the thick, soft curves of his mouth.

She had never really taken the lead. She could only imagine what people she knew might think if they saw her parading around in Safire's clothes and trying, as she was now, to entice this man. But she was happy to be having fun with Jeremy and being so unlike herself, having a life so unlike her life.

She wasn't sure what to do, but she ran her hands over his broad shoulders and down his hard chest and rippled abdomen. She scooted closer to him, close enough to press her chest against his and rub it back and forth, teasing herself and, she hoped, teasing him.

"I love what you're doing," he said. "You're so beautiful."

His words gave her the courage to continue, and she let the hand that had been caressing his chest move down over his belly again and then flutter over the front of his pants. He murmured and his thighs tensed, and she continued searching over his center until she found what she was looking for.

She ran her hand along his member until he writhed and brought one of his hands over hers to apply more pressure.

She claimed his lips again, pulling his hands to her breasts and then returning hers to his body. She felt her nipples harden under his fingers and heard a low groan in his throat. She moved her mouth from his lips to his ear and felt his manhood leap beneath her fingers.

"What are you doing to me?" he asked.

"I wanted to turn you on," she said with her lips moving over his ear.

He laughed. "You've succeeded wonderfully."

Angelina couldn't help smiling. He must have felt it because he ravaged her breasts with his fingers, making her moan.

She took his hands away and opened his shirt, dipping down to capture one of his nipples in her mouth while still toying with the front of his pants. He groaned and bucked against her fingers and mouth.

Being in control made her feel sexy. Heat and moisture

were flooding her center, and her womanhood was beginning to throb.

She stood for a moment and then straddled Jeremy's thighs, bringing herself over the thick ridge in his pants where she could feel it against her sex. She took off her belt and pulled her sheer cover-up over her head before bending forward to find his lips.

She started to rock, moaning into his mouth as the sensation of oscillating over his manhood filled her body with desire. Her chest heaved in his palms, and her hips tossed roughly. His buttocks clenched, raising him against her, and she almost lost control, sighing against his lips.

She got up suddenly and took his hand, drawing him inside.

He removed a condom from his wallet, and she took it from him and sat on the edge of her bed. She tugged at his pants and he removed them, along with his shorts and shoes and socks. His shirt hung open at his shoulders. She pulled on his sleeves and it slid to the floor.

She liked being the one who still had her clothes on for a change. And though she was hesitant about what she was going to do, the thrill of having control over his pleasure in this way—in a way she hadn't ever had before, hadn't ever done—overpowered any reluctance.

Angelina opened the package and took out the slippery disc, and as she rolled it down his member, she bent her head to follow its path. Jeremy moaned when her warm lips touched him. His thighs tensed as she lowered her head, and he thrust forward gently, bringing his hands to her shoulders. She continued until he sucked in his breath and pulled away from her.

She sat up, her hands coming together in front of her chest. Had she done something wrong?

He must have seen the question in her eyes.

"It was perfect, Safire, too perfect."

She wanted to correct him about her name. She'd forgotten until now. But now didn't seem the time. Maybe it should wait until they were back on land.

She stood and was swept into his arms, into his kiss.

When they broke apart, she turned around and lifted her hair so that he could unzip her dress, then she guided him onto the bed and stopped to remove the garment and her shoes and underwear.

When Angelina turned to the bed, Jeremy's eyes were upon her, glazed over with lust.

She climbed onto the bed and threw her leg over him, straddling him again, but this time there was nothing to separate them except his thin sheath. She moved over him and felt a tingle run through her center and into her body.

"I love the feel of you this way," she said.

"So do I," he answered. "I can't wait for more."

He leaned up on one of his elbows and took one of her breasts into his mouth. She cried out with pleasure and ground against the length of him. They were in the darkness this time, and the darkness seemed to act as a shield, spurring Angelina onward.

She touched his manhood and brought it against her, running herself along it. Jeremy fell back against the pillow groaning and thrust upward toward her. She raised herself and lowered herself onto him, swirling her hips until he moaned again. She loved having the control.

She lowered her torso to rake her breasts across his chest and to savor his lips with her own. Then she sat up and braced her hands on his chest. He cupped both of her breasts in one of his palms and began to tease her nipples. Without thinking, she tilted her hips and oscillated along his sex. He groaned again.

"You're amazing," he said.

With that brief reassurance, she started to move along his body, consuming them both with fire. His fingers were still teasing her breasts, and he filled her completely. When he added the pressure of his other hand over her sex as she moved along him, she found herself coursing toward the edge, spurred on by the sensations running through her body.

Before long, her sex clamped onto his and waves of muscular spasms shattered through her. She cried out just as he moaned, his body tensing beneath hers and then starting to shake.

She collapsed on top of him, trying to catch her breath, and hid her face in the crook of his neck. He rubbed her hair, breathing heavily.

"Did I tell you that you're amazing?" he asked and tickled her sides.

She laughed and rolled next to him but not out of reach. He kissed her smile and tugged her into his arms.

"Just so you know," he said, "the night isn't over yet."

Chapter 8

Jeremy stood under the shower's spray and stretched. The warm water eased the tension in his neck and shoulders from swimming.

It was their last day on the ship, and they would be at sea all day. There were any number of things to do, but mainly, Jeremy wanted to have the time with Safire, and he knew she felt the same way. After breakfast, they went to one of the pools for their last chance to swim onboard.

They had gone back to their rooms to shower and dress for the afternoon. It was the first time they'd been apart all day. He sure was going to miss this woman—as early as tomorrow. But that wouldn't last long. They were having breakfast in the morning to exchange information before disembarking. She had no idea how soon he'd be showing up at her door.

He chuckled to himself and stepped out of the spray. He dressed and then called Alistair to see what time they were on for dinner and where. It was the last night, so they had all decided to go out together after the meal. Safire and Verniece were included in the group. Meanwhile, he wasn't sure what they'd be doing for the afternoon.

He needn't have worried. When he got to her cabin door, she greeted him in a blue calf-length eyelet skirt with a matching shirt that went over a white tank top. She had on her one-inch sandals with the wooden heels and had her purse over her shoulder ready to head down the hall, but he suddenly had other ideas.

When he pulled her into his arms, she laughed, kissing him, and then put an arm up between them.

"We're ready to go."

"But you don't even know where we're going, do you?"

"Well, no. Do you?"

"No."

They both laughed.

"While you're deciding what we should do," he said, taking the eyelet shirt from her shoulders, "I'll be right here."

He kissed the back of her shoulder and followed a pathway up to her neck until a shiver ran through her body.

When she turned to him, her lips were greedy for his. It was the first time since they'd been seeing each other that she'd let herself go so easily. She was a woman who wanted him, and that turned him on as much as anything else could.

They had started to know each other's bodies. He knew where to touch her to make her shiver, where to put his mouth to make her wet and where to put pressure to make her moan. But there was still so much that they hadn't done, and today he wanted to do some of those things.

He nibbled her breasts through her tank top until the nipples were hard, then he moved his hand under her skirt to play between her legs until he could feel her moisture on his fingertips. When he turned her toward the table and pulled her panties down, positioning himself behind her, she was startled for a moment, but then she moved with him, her eyes glazing over with desire.

Then she took one of his hands from her breasts and moved it to her sex, pressing it against her as she rocked up and down. It made her sigh. It made her grip the table to steady herself. He was on the verge of exploding, and they had only just started.

"Is this okay?" she asked.

"You never have to ask that, honey."

They spent the afternoon making love. In his book, it

was the best time they'd had, not because of anything that they did but because of the raw passion between them. And because Safire seemed freer than any other time. She was always responsive, but today she finally seemed to let herself go.

When she showered and put her clothes back on, it was hard for him to imagine that she was the woman who'd been so sensual and erotic a few minutes before. Her hair was pulled back into a ponytail, adding a youthful innocence to her look. Her calf-length skirt made her seem more staid and conservative.

It was when she looked at him and smiled that he could see the wilder woman beneath the tamed exterior. And it was when she tilted her head up and kissed him gently on the lips that he knew she was the same, sensuous woman.

They had dinner at the Bird of Paradise Restaurant.

"Okay," he said. "You got all my embarrassing moments from my friends. What about yours?"

"No, no. It doesn't work that way. People don't voluntarily offer up their worst moments. You have to get that from my friends and family members."

"But that's not fair. You're here alone."

She shrugged and then smiled. She wasn't giving up the goods.

He smiled back, making a mental note to grill her family when he met them.

"Do you go right back to work when you get back?" she asked.

"Yes, I do. I wish I had another week, but I'm back the day after tomorrow."

"So am I. We better make the best of tonight."

"Wait," he said. "Does that mean we should play or that we should rest?"

"I don't know. Which do you prefer?"

"I know you're not asking me. I always vote to play."

He reached for her hand across the table and stroked her fingers in a tell-tale manner. She drew back her hand and swatted at his knuckles.

"We just did that all afternoon. You're not ready for more, are you?"

"With you, I'm always ready for more. But we can meet the crew and do something else first, if you'd like."

"First?"

Just the thought of having her again made his body start to get hot.

"Yes, that can be second."

"Would your friends want to go to the theater? We haven't been yet. Not for an actual play."

"If not, we can go together. What's showing? Can we get tickets at this point?"

"I'll have to check and see. I'll do that after we eat. I need to make a call anyway."

They finished their meals and started to part.

"Should I come with you?" he asked.

"No, I'll only be a few minutes."

It was no longer strange to him that he wanted to go with her, would rather be with her than hanging out with his boys.

He met the guys in the Tiki Lounge. Safire and Verniece weren't there as yet, so for a few minutes, it was just him, Alistair, Myron and Rudy. They were already seated at the bar and had started in on a round of margaritas.

"Where is she?" Alistair asked, swiveling on his stool to face Jeremy's direction. "We haven't finished our conversation."

"She's coming," Jeremy replied and signaled the bartender so that he could order a margarita.

"We haven't seen hide nor hair of you this trip," Rudy said.

"And we all know why," Myron added.

"You hush," Alistair said to Myron. "We've hardly seen you, either."

Jeremy, Rudy and Alistair laughed. Myron turned shamefaced, acknowledging his absence from the group to be with Verniece.

"You shouldn't be laughing," Rudy said to Jeremy. "We haven't seen you *at all*."

Jeremy found a bar stool and hiked his leg up. His margarita arrived and was placed on the counter before him.

"And with good reason," Jeremy said.

"He's made a love connection," Rudy said and laughed.

"That's not the only thing they've connected," Myron said.

"Yeah," Rudy added, turning to Myron, "You said he had his tongue in her mouth the first time they kissed."

Jeremy didn't like the direction of the conversation. He nodded grimly and put down his drink.

"Okay," he said. "That's going a little too far."

"But it's true," Myron said.

Rudy gave Myron a high five. "I want to be like Mike," Rudy said. He was leading the charge to make fun of Jeremy and dragging Myron along with him. Unfortunately, Myron was willing to follow the lead.

"Wait," Myron said. "Alistair has the listing."

Alistair held up both his hands and shook his head, taking himself out of the ruckus, but Rudy grabbed the brochure on the bar in front of him.

"She's looking for a man who thinks he can tame her urges with tender loving care. She's a bit risqué. Oh, she's a sensual woman who knows what she wants and isn't afraid to get it. She's naughty and nice."

Jeremy didn't like them laughing over Safire's bio, but he knew that once they were started, it would take them a minute to cool down. Then he would have a few choice words for them. He decided to leave the group for a little while. He could come back in a few minutes when they'd gotten the message.

But when he swung his leg down from the stool and turned around, there she was. She'd been standing behind them for who knows how long. The crushed look on her face said that she'd heard enough.

Before he could say anything, she had turned away and started off.

"Safire," he called after her and beat a path to follow her. "Safire, it's not what it might have sounded like. The guys were just being idiots to tease me."

She didn't slow down. He tried to grab her arm, but she shook herself free from his grasp and stomped on.

"Don't touch me."

"Safire, I wasn't participating in their conversation. They were just ribbing me, and they went too far."

She had to wait for the elevator. He tried to take hold of her shoulders, but she waved her pocketbook at him furiously.

"Don't touch me."

He boarded the elevator with her and then pursued her down to her room. She tried to slam the door in his face once she got inside, but his foot was already in the door so he followed her into the room.

"Safire, don't make too much of this. They were wrong, but it was me they were kidding with, not you."

Safire went to her desk and rifled through a stack of brochures for the cruise. When she found the one for singles, she flipped through the pages until she came to her bio. He saw tears spring into her eyes as she started reading.

"This is what you thought I was, isn't it? You read this before we even met, didn't you?"

"Yes, I did, but I was only trying to find your name so that I could see you again."

"So you didn't think I was the one who made this up?"

She was trying to rope him into seeming like a bastard.

"I didn't know what to think. I only wanted to see you again."

"You thought I was just some hoochie mama. You were looking for a booty call, and that's what you and your boys think you found, huh?"

"Safire, it's not like that, and you know it."

"I know what I heard, and I didn't hear you say anything about it."

"Once they get started—"

"That's why you invited me back to your place the second time we met, isn't it? You thought I was just a tramp, an easy fling. Why else would you invite me back to your cabin before we knew anything about each other? Get out."

There were tears streaming down her face.

"Safire, you're not being fair. Hear me out."

"I can't believe I let this happen to me. And I just went along with it, being reckless and wild." She cringed for a moment, covering herself with her hands. "And you were part of this, having yourself one hell of a time. And just when I was starting to trust you and let…go with you."

"Safire, I never intended to—"

"No, you were just doing what the ad said. Right?"

"I wasn't following any ad, Safire."

"It's how you knew my name. You read it."

"You're turning this into something it wasn't," he said, "and you don't know me the way I thought you were getting to know me."

"Well, you don't know me at all. You should leave."

"We should talk about this."

She read over the bio again, shaking her head. Tears were still running down her face, but her expression was resigned, jaded. "This is what you thought of me. You should go."

"Safire—"

"Please go."

There was no reasoning with her right now, so he headed toward the door.

"When you calm down and remember that I'm not the one responsible for what the ad says and that I'm not the one who was kidding about it, call me."

He was frustrated enough to slam her door, and his next stop was going to be his so-called friends. Alistair was more mature; he hadn't participated. But Myron and Rudy were soon to be off his list. Still, their joshing wasn't meant for her ears; they were just guys. She had blown that out of proportion and wouldn't give him a chance to explain otherwise.

When he got back to the Tiki Lounge, the guys were apologetic. He was still angry with them and said so, but he knew from the looks on their faces that it wouldn't happen again.

Safire was another question. He went back to his room, but she wouldn't answer his calls. He even went to her door to knock, but she didn't answer.

Back in his room, Jeremy tried to calm down and see it from her point of view. She obviously had never seen the bio before, so she hadn't written it, and it did make her out to be...well, in his words, sexually empowered. But she wouldn't see it that way. She'd see it as making her out to be slutty.

That wasn't why he was attracted to her or why he had acted on that attraction, but she wouldn't give him a chance to explain.

He tried to read a bit, but it didn't work. They should have been at the theater by now. He waited a while and called her again, but again she didn't respond.

He went to bed early, hoping that she would be cooled off by breakfast and would come. That's when they would be exchanging information, working out how they'd keep seeing each other once they got back home.

In the morning, however, there was no sign of her at the restaurant they had chosen, and by the time he got to her stateroom, the maid service was cleaning it out. She had already gone.

Chapter 9

Her cousin Alex picked Angelina up at the Port of Miami earlier than they had first arranged, too early, as far as he was concerned. His days generally began at noon, unless he had a job interview, which was getting rarer and rarer these days.

Angelina was still distraught over the fiasco with Jeremy. She couldn't believe what she'd let happen, what she'd done. Being someone's booty call wasn't her idea of a way to have fun. She knew her sister would call her a prude, but so be it.

She wanted to have a word with her sister about that ad and about letting her skip onto the ship without knowing what it said. In a real way, her sister had set her up for what had happened. Only Safire didn't know Angelina would be going when she submitted that bio. Even if Safire had wanted to get her a few dates, she wouldn't have said those things.

But she couldn't tell Safire about the problem with that ad without having to tell her about what had happened with Jeremy also. She would have to admit to being reckless and wild with a stranger. Ironically, her sister would probably be glad for her, but that wasn't the example she wanted to set.

As inappropriate as the ad was for Angelina, she had to admit that Safire would never have gotten herself into that kind of mess. If Safire wanted something casual, it would be casual. If she wanted something serious, she could have that, too. She would never have let herself be the butt of the joke shared by a group of guys.

In the end, she didn't begrudge her sister her sexual liberation, so it wasn't worth mentioning. Now, if only she could forget the incident and get on with her life. It was just so hard to believe that after all that time they'd spent together, she amounted to a sex toy to him. She couldn't imagine what her friends would say if they knew. She shuddered and tried to put the thought from her mind.

When they got home, Angelina unpacked and distributed the presents she'd gotten. The coral necklace was for her great-aunt, who admired it with palsied fingers and then got her walker to go put it in a napkin. The silver chains with ship pendants on them were for Philly and Alex. She put Philly's on for him. At six, he was excited with just about anything.

The handheld game was for Philly with instructions to let Alex teach him how to use it. Alex was twenty, and he would have as much fun with it as Philly would, so they could share it. The bracelet was for Safire, who didn't live with them, so she would have to get her gift later.

It was Sunday, so Angelina had her regular errands to run—grocery store, bulk food store, pharmacy, discount store. Then she needed to braid her great-aunt's hair, set her medicines out for the week, and get her clothes out for the next morning. She needed to wash and set her own hair. Then she could pull out something for work the next day that would cover up her tan, which didn't fit with her sober work clothes. And she was there in time to make lunch and dinner.

She would be up all night finishing her three syllabi, but at least she would be able to post them online and take them to the copy place in the morning so that they would be ready for classes. After that, she could figure out a schedule for getting her article done and working on her novel.

Next week, Philly was back to school, so she wouldn't have to rely on Alex and Aunt Rose as much to keep their eyes on him while she was at work. And her great-aunt needed attention herself, so Alex had been doing double duty over the last nine days—with Safire's help.

Now it was up to her again, and the cruise seemed almost like a dream—a cruel one at that. Playtime was over, and now she had to play catch-up.

By the next afternoon, Angelina was starting to feel the drain of the constant running around. By the end of the week, she was running on automatic.

"You have five more minutes to finish your paragraph on chapter then of Frederick Douglass's *Narrative*. Homework for Monday is to finish reading Douglass's autobiography and to read chapter one in *History of the Black Atlantic*."

Students began handing in their paragraphs. Angelina smiled as she took each one and began packing up her books and notes.

She had the next period for office hours, but it was too early in the term for anyone to come in, so she busied herself checking email. Just then, her thoughts ran to the cruise and to him.

She still hadn't been able to rid her mind of Jeremy, but here in her real workaday life, thoughts of him were simply interruptions of fantasy into reality. They usually started with a time that they had made love or had spent together, but they always ended with her shame and embarrassment—with her being the butt of his friends' jokes. It was just starting to get easier to shake them off and get back to real life.

She worked at her desk for an hour and a half, then she packed up for the day and headed to her car. She stopped for a few items at the grocery store and then drove home.

When she got there, she went to Philly's room to check on him.

"Hey, pumpkin."

He was playing a car racing game on the computer, and unlike most other days, he came and greeted her with a hug.

"Hi."

She squeezed him and rubbed his head, wondering what prompted the hug.

"Game not going well?"

"Yeah, it's fine."

She held his head and looked into his eyes; he seemed okay.

"Well, I'll go start dinner. Spaghetti and meatballs sound good?"

"Yep. Can I help?"

She held his shoulder and put the back of her hand to his forehead. "You don't have a fever. You feeling okay?" She chuckled.

"Yep."

Philly had been hovering a little closer to her the past week, and now she realized that it was because he had missed her.

"Okay, let's go get dinner ready."

"I get to make...the balls."

"That's perfect," she said and picked him up.

With spaghetti in the strainer, meatballs simmering in the sauce, rolls heating in the oven and salad waiting in a big wooden bowl, Angelina turned from the kitchen.

"Alex, come set the table and get the drinks. I'll get Aunt Rose."

Upstairs, she peeked in on her great-aunt, who was sitting up in bed and watching the soaps on television.

"Dinner's ready."

"Oh, good, honey."

Her great-aunt reached for her false teeth and began the process of repositioning herself on the bed so that she could get up. Angelina moved her great-aunt's walker next to the bed within her reach.

"I'll be right back to go downstairs with you."

Angelina was glad to finally get out of her shoes and made a quick change into sweatpants. She already missed the days when she didn't have to worry about getting dinner ready, when all she had to do was figure out what time she would meet...

By the time she returned, her great-aunt's feet were on the floor. She took the older woman's hands and let her pull herself up to a standing position. Going downstairs, Aunt Rose had to take one step at time, but she was okay on her own once she got to the bottom.

"Did you find any job leads today?" Angelina asked Alex over dinner.

"I found a couple things in the paper."

"Don't forget that school is an option."

He had gone to Howard, where you still had to take swimming, which brought his average down....

"I know," Alex said.

"Thank you for watching Philly today. I owe you. Are you guys still playing with that handheld game?"

"Yeah, it's cool."

Alex wasn't one of many words, and Angelina didn't know how else to get him talking, so she patted his hand briefly and turned to her great-aunt.

"How was your day, Aunt Rose?"

"Oh, the same. Knees still aching a bit."

"We have to talk to the doctor about that again."

He was a radiologist. He would know a boatload of doctors and nurses and...

"Nothing to do for it more than I am," her great-aunt said. "It comes and goes. Ms. Lee stopped by this afternoon with some lunch for me. I already ate with Phillip and Alexander, so it's in there for tomorrow."

Ms. Lee was her great-aunt's best friend. She lived a block over in the retirement village.

"Is there anything going on at the retirement center you want to go to?"

"Nothing right now. There's a new pastor coming that they're having to the center a few weeks from now that Ms. Lee was telling me about. I'd like to see him when he comes."

"What day is it? Sunday?"

That's the day they were to meet for breakfast and exchange numbers so that they...

"I think a Wednesday. I'll check."

"Let me know so that I can be sure I can take you."

"I'll get the news from Ms. Lee when she comes by again."

"Okay. I'll be available." Angelina turned to Philly, "What about you, sweetie? Are you ready for school next week?"

"Uh-ha. It was supposed to be this week. But they're doing stuff to the school."

"I know. They're renovating. I have a list of supplies we need to get this week. You coming with me?"

"Yes."

"Then we can get some school clothes for you while we're out. Do you need anything, Alex?"

"No, I'm fine."

"No clothes?"

Maybe some polo shirts would look good on him, like the ones she'd picked for...

"No, I'm fine on clothes."

Angelina wasn't sure he would tell her if he did need something.

"You'll let me know when you do?"

"Yeah."

Angelina dipped the remainder of her bread into the last bit of sauce on her plate.

Like their first meal together, when he put his hand on the back of her chair and stroked her shoulder....

Tonight everything reminded her of Jeremy. She couldn't shake that cruise from her mind, and she couldn't stop her heart from feeling broken. But she didn't have time for this—for wallowing.

"Speaking of clothes, I need your laundry when we're done."

While Alex and Philly stacked the dishwasher, Angelina got her great-aunt into the living room and did the heavy dishes in the sink. Then she got her aunt's laundry while Philly and Alex collected theirs. She got the first load in while Alex found something on the television that he, Philly and Aunt Rose could watch together.

With a third load in the laundry, she collected Aunt Rose and helped her up the stairs and into her nightclothes. Next it was Philly's turn. After he got his teeth brushed and his pajamas on, she read to him while the third load dried. The little one dropped off to sleep before she had to go check the dryer.

When that load was done, she said good-night to Alex and left him downstairs watching television. She finally had some time to get some of her own work done.

She had two work stations in her room—one for the computer and one for paperwork. She took a seat at the table she used for writing and stared at the piles on it, trying to weigh them. It was her usual balancing act, but it caused her a great deal of anxiety.

The papers to grade and the books for class prep needed to be done for Monday. The research she'd collected for her critical article and the draft of what she'd done so far on her novel were less pressing, but it was the latter to which she was drawn. She knew she couldn't spend that much time with her creative writing, so she decided that she would only read over the last few chapters for editing and changes.

The time that she'd spent working on the ship had been split between her syllabi, her reading and her creative writing. They had actually gotten equal time. The creative writing was a luxury, but it seemed to match with the extravagance of being on a cruise. Now she didn't have that leisure.

Of course, the whole cruise had been on borrowed time. She'd taken work with her to do, but hadn't gotten enough of it done, so now she had to make up for that, too. She hadn't anticipated those warm brown eyes, those strong brown arms, those hard brown thighs...

Angelina pulled herself back to reality. She had been thinking about making love to Jeremy on the cruise, before everything went sour. And she couldn't afford to let her mind wander to what she couldn't have. It just made her desirous to no end. Then she would be let down. It was like waking from a dream that you want to recapture but just can't. The day has to begin. Real life is different.

She had replayed that last evening in her mind over and over. Listening to his friends paint her as a loose hussy, listening to their laughter, watching him do and say nothing, knowing what he had wanted her for, knowing that he had gotten just that—it all mortified her, debased her. What had she been thinking? Or rather, why hadn't she been thinking?

And here she was again, mulling over what she had deliberately put out of her mind and wasting time in the process.

She finished reading over the last few pages of her draft and then turned to class preparation for Monday. She already knew Douglass's *Narrative* and had lecture notes on that, so she started reading *History of the Black Atlantic*.

She hoped that when she was done with her reading,

she would be able to start on the papers or do some notes for her article. By the time she closed the book, however, it was past midnight, and she was exhausted.

She changed for bed, aware that her modest cotton pajamas were a far cry from the silk concoctions that she'd worn on the Palace of the Seas. Who really wore such things in real life? Well, Safire did. But who else?

Tomorrow was Saturday. She had her usual errands to run, plus school supplies and clothes for Philly to get. She also wanted to find something to thank Alex for helping during her time away, and she needed to see if the pharmacist could recommend anything for Aunt Rose's knees. She also needed to get her lecture notes done and to get started on the papers.

Yes, she was back to real life.

Chapter 10

Jeremy opened his desk, realized that he wasn't looking for anything and slammed it shut.

"Dr. Bell?"

"Yes, Evelyn, come in. Do you need anything?"

"Dr. Carter is on the phone. He's wondering when he'll have the results of the MRI on patient Watson."

"Tell him— No, just put him through."

He rifled on his desk for a file and picked up the phone when it rang.

"Hello, James. We just finished with Ms. Watson and her son. I can get the write-up done tomorrow morning and fax it to you. Do you want preliminary findings now, or do you want to wait?"

Jeremy opened the file and gave James Carter the preliminary findings. It refocused him, and when he put the phone down, he was centered and cool.

He was also a bit pissed off. Safire was on his mind again, and once again, he couldn't see her reasons for ditching him the last day of the cruise, when they were to have had breakfast and exchanged information. He understood her being a bit miffed for a little while, maybe an evening, but to cut him out of her life completely over some kidding that he wasn't even participating in—it was too much.

He replaced the file and took off his lab coat. He pulled out his shorts and jersey to get ready to meet Alistair for racquetball.

He also had plans to meet some friends that evening for

dinner and a club, but he was thinking about calling to beg off. It meant trying to show interest in other women when he couldn't muster the energy, and it meant pretending to be at ease when he couldn't stop thinking about Safire.

He stopped and sat down at his desk. He'd started to do it earlier in the day but hadn't had time between clients. He logged onto his computer and did an online search for Safire Lewis. Her name popped up just like that. Safire Lewis. She was a paralegal in the law offices of Benson and Hines. What? No, he needed Safire Lewis the history teacher.

He clicked on the paralegal's name, and once he found the right page, there she was. It was another small picture, but it was Safire, looking just as she did in the singles brochure. She had on a wide straw hat and a sundress, and she was standing on a dock in front of a motorboat, waving.

He flipped through the other images. Everyone else had on a business suit, and all the men wore ties. Why would she put a vacation picture next to her job profile? It seemed unlike Safire. But then, she seemed to be a history teacher; she had even brought history books with her on vacation. It didn't even make for a plausible lie. Being a history teacher didn't make her more attractive.

He was confused, but he wouldn't be for long. He printed the page and picked up the phone.

"I'm trying to get in touch with Ms. Safire Lewis."

"I'm sorry. She's gone for the day. Can I take a message?"

"Is she in tomorrow?"

"Yes, sir."

"What would be a good time to catch her?"

"She may be assisting at court in the morning. Try around three o'clock."

"Will do. Thank you."

Jeremy hung up the phone. Then, on an impulse, he picked it up again.

"Hello? Tom?…Yeah. This is Jeremy Bell. I'm glad to catch you. I'm wondering if you can cover for me for a few hours tomorrow. I have one CT scan…That's great. I'll owe you one…Actually, I can do that. That's perfect. It's a trade. I need to be out at two…Great."

He wanted to go out and unwind, but he decided against it. He cancelled clubbing plans for that night, and then he changed to meet Alistair.

He and Alistair were both pretty athletic, but they had been going at it for a while and were winding down. He didn't stop, though; he could keep going as long as his friend. They had slowed down enough to start talking, and it was Alistair who brought up the subject.

"So." Alistair hit the ball toward the wall. "You're still thinking about her?"

Jeremy missed the return. "Yeah, I guess so."

Alistair put the ball in play again, and Jeremy returned it.

"You gonna do anything about it?"

"I did an online search. I'm going to pay her a visit tomorrow."

"All right," Alistair said, missing the ball and stopping, "a man of action. Is she expecting you?"

Jeremy retrieved the ball and put it in play again. "No."

Alistair made the return. "Ouch. That might not be nice."

"I'll have to see. And it's not a conversation I want to have by phone."

"I understand. Let me know how it goes."

Jeremy stopped the ball. "I will."

"Reggie and I are going to do Chinese," Alistair said. "Join us."

"No, spend time with your partner."

"I always do. It's not a special occasion. Come with us."

"Okay." Jeremy looked at his watch and handed Alistair the ball. "Let's go."

Dinner that night was among friends who kept him occupied, but work the next day was a test in patience. At two o'clock, though, he was on his way to his car and heading across town to the law offices of Benson and Hines.

A receptionist pointed him toward a back office, where he found a woman in a short, tight skirt and high heels behind a stack of law books.

"Hi," he said.

When she looked up, he could see that she looked a lot like Safire but that it wasn't her. She had Safire's features—her elliptical eyes, her full lips, her puckered cheekbones, her pert nose, her high forehead. Only she wasn't Safire. She was younger, for one thing, and a bit smaller, for another.

She eyed him up and down, checking his "package" along the way. "You *must* be looking for me."

She got up and extended her hand.

"No, I'm looking for Safire Lewis."

She smiled and sat down with her legs revealed in his direction.

"I knew you were looking for me."

She smiled sweetly. This one could be as raunchy as she wanted to be and get away with it; an air about her kept her in control and kept her from seeming common. He might have done a double take if he wasn't used to flirting with the Safires of the world, but he was.

And she was Safire. She was probably twenty-three, and right down to being "naughty but nice," everything the singles profile said about Safire resonated as true.

"You are Safire Lewis, aren't you? You fit the description you gave the singles cruise. But I'm looking for the woman who went instead of you."

She got up and crossed her arms like a blockade. She

was protecting her sister or cousin. Or it could have been a friend or a chance doppelgänger.

"Why would you be looking for her if she wanted to be found?"

Jeremy needed to get that blockade down, and being honest was the only way that he knew how.

"We spent almost every day together on the ship, and we'd still be seeing each other now if she hadn't found out… that I'd read your bio before I met her."

A light went off in her head and lit up her face with understanding.

"Uh-oh."

He wasn't sure if she said it because of his situation or because it was clear that her friend now knew about the profile.

"She was nothing like your bio, but I couldn't help being attracted to her."

She put her finger up. "Wait here a moment." She crossed the room, took out her purse, flipped open her phone and hit a number. Apparently, she got no answer, and she snapped it shut without leaving a message. Then she stood thinking.

"Look, Ms. Lewis, you obviously care about her. I wouldn't be here if I didn't care about her, too. We were together just about all the time. I can't let it go."

"What if you were a cruise ship affair to her, and she doesn't want to see you again?"

"She wasn't like that. It wasn't like that."

"Well, you seem to know something about her. Tell me more."

Jeremy took a breath and started with seeing her on the boarding ramp the first day, trying not to give details that his Safire probably wouldn't want to have known.

"We shopped and went to Magen's Bay when we got to St. Thomas. I joined her for the tour in Puerto Rico. She met some of my friends at one of the pools. We…spent time together aboard the ship—one of the gardens, a concert. What else do you need to know?"

"What did she bring me back?"

She was just being curious now, but she had the information he needed, so he had to play along.

"We went to a silver store on St. Thomas. It would be either the bracelet with the hibiscus or the necklace with coral beads, but I'll guess the bracelet."

Safire held out her hand and pulled up the cuff of her sleeve. There it was.

"And what about...the naughty?"

She was obviously snooping into her friend's business now. He gave her a wry look and remained silent. She sat back in her chair and laughed, clearly intrigued by the fact that his Safire had even *had* any naughty, as she put it. But it was also clear to her that she would get no information on that from him.

"Please tell me how I can reach her."

"You know, it's been a couple of weeks. Why the wait?"

"Honestly, I don't know." And he didn't. She had his cell phone number, but she hadn't used it. Maybe he'd just expected that she would call eventually, but now he couldn't wait. "I guess I expected her to call, seeing that she has my name and number. I didn't know what an impact that bio really had. And then I didn't know how to reach her—or you."

"You seem genuine. And you're gorgeous as hell." She laughed, weighing the issue in her mind. Then she turned to him. "You're looking for my sister, Angelina—Angelina Lewis."

Jeremy smiled at Safire. "Angelina Lewis. Thank you."

"I'll give you her number, but that's it. The rest is on you."

"I don't want to do this on the phone. I need to see her."

"Look, for all I know, you might be a stalker. You're lucky you're getting this much."

He held up his hands.

"Okay. Okay, I'll make do."

Safire wrote her sister's name and number on a legal pad and handed Jeremy the page. "But if it doesn't work out, the real Safire is right here." She gave him a wink.

"You are a vixen, aren't you? We might have to do something about that. We can't let baby sister fall in with the wrong crowd."

"Ah. Now you sound like you've spent time with my sister."

She laughed, and he crossed the room to give her a brief, thankful hug.

"I'll be seeing you again," he said.

"We'll see. No promises."

Jeremy left the office elated, but he was also a bit perturbed. Why hadn't she ever told him the truth, at least about her real name? After what they had shared, that was the minimum they should know about one another. He remembered her starting to say something about her name. Clearly, she had changed her mind.

He got on his BlackBerry as soon as he closed his car door. His reverse search turned up nothing, so she probably only had a cell phone number, but his online search brought her right up. Angelina Lewis was an assistant professor in the Department of History at Florida International University. And there she was—his Safire.

It was almost three, but he wasn't far from FIU and decided to take a chance that she might still be there. He found the building without too much trouble, parked illegally and went in.

He found her in her office alone, checking her email. She had on a long skirt and a loose blouse with a bow hanging down from her neck. She shut down the computer and began loading her books, getting ready to leave.

It startled her when she saw him standing at her door.

Something in her face opened momentarily and then snapped shut in anger.

"What are you doing here?"

"I needed to see you again."

She started packing up her books again. "Haven't you had enough of a laugh at my expense?"

"That's still not fair. I wasn't laughing. I wasn't pleased, either." He sat down in the chair next to her desk. "Safire—I mean Angelina. I apologize for my friends' stupidity. You're not like the bio. You haven't been from the start. That's not why I liked you."

"How did you find me?"

"First I found your sister—the real Safire Lewis."

She rolled her eyes and let her head fall back. "Now she knows about all this."

"She knows some things. She interrogated me before she would even give me your name or tell me that you were her sister. You do look a lot alike, but you're not alike. You know, you could have told me your real name. I'd have kept your secret."

"Whenever I thought about it, there were other people around or..."

He caught what was on her mind; it was when they were making love. He lowered his voice. "Or there wasn't anyone else around."

He saw a shiver run through her and knew that they had understood each other. He also knew that she was still attracted to him.

"I couldn't risk being caught using my sister's passport. I figured I would find the right time to tell you, or I'd tell you when we got back. I didn't know I was a...an amusement. I have to go."

"Please don't go yet."

"I have a pickup to make by four."

"Let me walk with you."

"There's nothing to talk about. We're in the real world now, not the world of fantasy romances. And whoever you thought I was, I'm clearly not. And now I have to explain this to my younger sister."

She grabbed her purse and snatched up her case.

"Have dinner with me. Let's talk about this. There *is* something to talk about—us."

Before she could leave her office and enter the well-travelled hall, he blocked her path. He touched her face, running his finger down her jaw to her chin. He saw her shiver again, and he knew he was breaking through her defenses—some of them.

But not all. She pushed his hand away and headed into the hall.

"Whatever you say, I won't believe you. I know what I heard and saw."

"*You* won't believe *me?* At least you knew my real name. I never lied to you or kept anything from you."

Wait. This was not how he wanted things to go.

"No, you and your friends just found a plaything. I can't be that anymore. This is real life, and I have obligations."

"I'm not asking you to be a plaything, and you know it."

"I know no such thing. I heard them joking with you over getting some. I read that ad."

"Your sister is the one who wrote that profile. And it's just like her, by the way. But it's not what drew me to you or what made me spend all of my time with you. That was you."

"You don't know me," she said, spitting out the words.

"I know enough to know that you liked me, too. You wanted me, too. That's—"

"Let's just say that I don't want you anymore and leave it at that."

They were at her car now, and she had put her things

in the backseat. She was getting behind the wheel, and he had no way to stop her.

"I'm sorry things turned out this way, but I have to go."

She turned on the engine, pulled out and drove off.

He'd never been so infuriated by a woman in his life. He'd tracked her down, had come to find her and had apologized for something that wasn't even his fault. And she'd just driven off. He wasn't used to getting turned down and certainly not when he was actually trying.

He got to his car in time to find a police officer giving him a ticket. He took it, got behind his own wheel and headed back across town to go home.

She wasn't even apologetic about not telling him who she was. *She* didn't believe *him*. Well, that was her choice.

By the time he flicked the remote for his garage, he was simmering. If she didn't want to believe him, fine. If she didn't want to talk things through, so be it. It she didn't want to be with him, good riddance.

Chapter 11

Angelina finished her eggs and sat with half a bagel on her plate. She was waiting for Aunt Rose to finish her oatmeal; then Angelina could help her into the living room. She was also waiting for Philly to finish his eggs so that she could get him to school. Alex came back from the fridge and poured more orange juice for himself and Philly.

"No more for me. Thank you." She turned to Philly. "Eat up, honey. We'll have to go soon."

"I'm almost done."

Angelina sighed. It had been several days since Jeremy's surprise visit, and she couldn't stop second-guessing herself. There was a moment during which her heart had leapt at the sight of him; then she remembered how it ended, and her joy came crashing down. He had sought her out, but he couldn't change what had happened. She wanted to believe him, but it would only mean degrading herself further.

Angelina got her great-aunt's pill organizer and emptied out the morning pills and supplements.

"All these pills," Aunt Rose said. "They do you more harm than good." But she took them.

When her great-aunt was finished, Angelina got up and took their plates and then wrapped up the rest of her bagel for lunch. Alex was already done and got Aunt Rose's walker, placing it next to her and holding it while she got up from the table.

Alex was such a godsend. He usually wore low-hanging jeans and scruffy T-shirts, looking like something the dog brought home. He generally went about with a cocky look, but he was a sweet kid—quiet to a fault but willing to pitch in and reluctant to ask for anything in return.

Philly was her little pumpkin. At six, he still had baby fat around the edges and the sweet, open face only a child can have. Soon it would start to elongate and get angular, but now his big brown eyes held the awe and wonder of youth and matched the high-pitched giggle he made when she tickled him.

She was about to quiz Philly on his homework when he announced that he was done.

"The bathroom's next," Angelina said. "And wash your hands."

She cleared the rest of the plates and glasses from the table, emptied them, and loaded them into the dishwasher. Then she got Philly's backpack, and when he returned, she helped him get it over his shoulders.

"This thing is almost bigger than you are. Is it too heavy, little one?"

"Nope."

"Okay. Well, let's see if Aunt Rose is settled, and then let's go."

Angelina went into the living room to check on her great-aunt, who was in front of the television. Alex was flipping the channels for her.

"Aunt Rose, are you okay?"

"Just fine, honey, just fine."

Philly had come in from the kitchen. Suddenly, though, he was on the floor.

Angelina ran to him. He was on top of his backpack. His eyes were closed, and his body was stiff.

"Philly? Philly, can you hear me?"

He didn't respond. Right under her hands, he began twitching and jerking violently. His arm hit hard against the foot of the couch, and Angelina put her hand between him and the couch to stop it from happening again. She pulled him out from against the couch, trying to figure out what to do.

"Alex. Alex. Call 911. No. It'll be quicker if I just take him. Run upstairs and get my purse."

Alex took the stairs two at a time.

"Aunt Rose, I need to take Philly to the hospital. Alex will stay with you."

Alex had returned, and they both stooped over Philly. When the convulsions stopped, he just lay there.

Alex picked him up. "I'm coming with you."

Angelina looked from her great-aunt to Alex. "Okay. Take him to the car and get in the backseat with him. Aunt Rose, we're taking Alex to the hospital. I'll call to let you know what's happening and when we'll be back. Will you be okay on your own for a little while?"

Her great-aunt was already waving her hands, ushering her out the door.

"Yes, dear, yes. Get the boy to the doctor."

"If we need to, I'll call Ms. Armstrong to see if she can come by."

"Go on, now, go on."

Angelina grabbed her purse and ran out the door.

Philly was still largely unresponsive when they brought him to the emergency room, so he was treated rather quickly.

"Has he had any other seizures that you know of?" the doctor asked.

"No. None."

"Has he had any fevers recently?"

"No, he's been fine."

"Describe what happened."

Angelina started describing the event, but she couldn't stop herself from growing emotional as she spoke. At the end, her voice was quavering, and there were tears in her eyes. "Then he just lay there."

"Has he had any infections recently?"

"No."

"Any blow to the head?"

"No, but I'm worried that he hit his arm when he was thrashing."

"Is he on any medications?"

"No. None."

"Do you have any family history of seizures?"

"No, not that I know of."

The doctor turned to Philly. "How old are you, Phillip?"

"Six."

"How is your arm?"

"It's okay."

"Does anything hurt?"

"No, ma'am."

She pointed a light at each of his eyes.

"Can you follow my fingers with your eyes?"

Philly followed her directions.

The doctor had been writing in her chart. She looked at it and then turned to Angelina. "Well, Ms. Lewis, what you described is a seizure, and he's recovering from it fairly quickly. There are lots of reasons that children have seizures—infections, medications, poisons, even unknown causes.

"What we're going to do now is draw some blood to check his sugar, his sodium and so on. I'll also look at his arm. If all the blood work comes back okay, we're going to send you to your regular doctor for a referral to a neurologist."

"Could it be epilepsy?" Angelina asked.

"One incident is too soon to tell. The neurologist will run a series of tests to find out. All of that will happen before any diagnosis is made or any medication is recommended for seizures. In the meantime, I'm going to give you some information on what to do if a seizure recurs, and I'll give you an extra copy for his teacher. If he has another one before he's seen by his regular doctor and a neurologist, bring him back to the E.R."

It was all a lot to take in. The blood tests came back normal, and Angelina was given a copy to take to their doctor. She called Philly's doctor, who was able to see him that afternoon.

Her classes met on Mondays, Wednesdays, and Fridays. Luckily, today was Tuesday. She had spent the morning in the hospital; she got Philly to his pediatrician that afternoon. They were set to see a pediatric neurosurgeon the following Tuesday and told to watch for additional seizures.

Alex was a sweetheart throughout the whole thing—holding Philly after he got out of the E.R., keeping Aunt Rose company while Philly saw Dr. Wilson. She hugged him tightly at the end of the night. She had been worried that he wasn't getting his life together, but now she also saw that when he felt needed, he stepped up to the task. If he could get it together, he would be a valuable young man.

Dr. James Carter was a pediatric neurologist at Miami Children's Hospital in South Miami. They lived in North Miami, so it wasn't one of the facilities near her home, but Dr. Wilson said he was one of the best, and Philly needed the best.

She'd never been to Miami Children's Hospital, but she was there the following Tuesday with Philly in tow. Alex had come to keep them company. She was sensing that he cared for Philly. He'd been keeping a closer eye on Philly since the first seizure, and he wanted to come to the doctor with them. Ms. Armstrong would look in on Aunt Rose that afternoon, which she usually only did when Angelina was in school.

There had been another episode, and she'd taken him

back to the E.R., but it was the same as the first time: he recovered after a little while, and all the blood tests came back normal. That was Saturday. Since he already had an appointment to see a neurologist, they sent him home.

Dr. Carter seemed competent and ordered a series of immediate tests for Philly. It was a good thing she'd planned on spending the day because they'd be there for most of it. The first stop was for an MRI scan of the brain. They expected a wait, so Alex took Philly onto his lap, saving a seat for her, while she went to the registration table to sign in.

Angelina was stunned to see Jeremy come out in a lab coat and call Philly's name. Apparently, he was just as surprised to see her and to see Philly climb down from Alex's lap, go to her and take her hand.

She hadn't planned to see Jeremy again and not here. She felt exposed and hoped that Philly and Alex didn't notice anything. There was a flutter in the pit of her stomach— nerves. But why? It was over.

At first she didn't know how to react. Then, knowing that it was for Philly and that there was no way to avoid the contact, she simply stepped toward Jeremy.

"He's right here. And you're a radiologist."

"A neuroradiologist, yes. Follow me."

After some brief questions, Jeremy, Dr. Bell, called in his assistant and handed her Philly's referral sheet and chart.

"Evelyn, please prep young Mr. Lewis for his MRI. I'll be in shortly. See you in a minute, kiddo."

Jeremy smiled at Philly but glared at her. Well, such was life. Fairy tales happened in romance novels and on cruise ships. In real life, you had to suck in your gut and keep going. And Philly needed this so that they could know what was wrong.

She followed the technician, who handed her some paperwork. Then they had Philly take off everything and get into a small hospital gown. He was placed on the table leading to the large machine, and they put supports on either side of his head to keep it from moving. She was allowed to stay with him there until the doctor, Jeremy, came back. Then she was called to the adjoining room.

"It'll be okay, Philly. You just hold still for as long as they tell you to hold still. Okay?"

"Do you have to leave?" Philly asked.

"I'll be right in the next room where I can see you and hear you the whole time. Okay, sweetie?"

"Okay."

She kissed his forehead and patted his hair before leaving his side. The test took some time, but Jeremy and his staff were soothing. It was clear that they were used to dealing with children.

She had done her best to put Jeremy out of her mind after he had come to see her at school, but she hadn't succeeded. He had been apologetic, but she couldn't bring herself to trust him, not even though his visit had spurred her dreams. She had even considered that maybe she'd been too hard on him, but confronted with real life, she thought it best to trust her intuition.

Now she had confirmation that she'd been right. Sweet as his voice sounded when he spoke to Philly, his cold stares were just as hard when he glanced her way.

After the test was over, she helped Philly get dressed and put the silver chain with the ship back around his neck. She gave him a hug and lifted him to her hip.

"You did really well, little one," Angelina said.

Philly put his head on her shoulder and closed his eyes. Staying still for so long had made him groggy. In the waiting area, she handed him back to Alex.

"The test is over."

"Do they know what it is yet?" Alex asked.

"I don't know. I'll check."

Just as she turned around, Jeremy called her back to his office.

"Do you know what's wrong yet?"

"I thought you didn't have any children."

"I need to know what's wrong, Jeremy, not rehash the past."

"I also thought you weren't involved? Or did you just find him? Isn't he a little young as well?"

"Jeremy, you're being childish. Tell me if you know what's wrong."

"I noted no overt abnormalities, but I'll do a careful reading of the scans. I'll also compare it with the EEG. It will be a few days before I'm able to submit the final report."

"A few days?"

"Why did you lie, Saf— Angelina, why did you lie? Was everything about you a lie?"

"You don't know anything about my life."

"Apparently so. I wasn't even given your real name."

Angelina gritted her teeth together and remained silent. She needed Jeremy's expertise to find out what was wrong with her brother. He could leap to whatever conclusions he wanted, and he could insult her as much as he wanted, as long as he did his job—the one he loved so much.

There were tears welling up at the back of her eyes, but she wouldn't give in to them. Yes, she was back to the real world now, and this was part of it.

There was a knock at the door.

"Yes," Jeremy answered.

Only it wasn't for him. Alex popped his head through the door.

"He's having another seizure."

Jeremy picked up the phone. "Call Dr. Carter for Phillip Lewis. Tell him the seizure is in progress, and see if he can come."

Angelina ran out to the waiting area where Philly was on the floor jerking violently.

"Philly? Philly, honey?"

A technician brought a gurney over, and Jeremy pulled her out of the way while the technicians raised Philly from the floor to the stretcher and secured the straps around his jerking limbs.

When he let her go, she went directly to Philly's side.

"Philly? It's okay, baby. The doctors are here."

Alex was on the other side of the stretcher looking stricken, and Angelina became aware that tears were streaming down her own face. She blotted at them with her palm, keeping one hand on Philly's head.

The technicians stayed at Philly's side until the convulsions stopped. Then he just lay there. Dr. Carter came in and recommended against medication to stop the seizure as Philly was resting quietly. Angelina held Philly's hand and motioned for Alex to come around to her. She patted Alex's back for a moment.

"Don't worry. They can take care of him here."

She said it as much for herself as for him.

"Take him to 142 until Carla gets here." It was Jeremy directing the technicians. When Angelina turned to look at him, he was heading back to his office.

They wheeled Philly to a room to get him out of the middle of the waiting area. Since the seizure appeared to be over, they left her and Alex alone with him.

"They didn't see anything right away on the MRI," Angelina said, patting Philly's arm. "They're going to check the scans again and send the results in a few days."

"Where do we go next?"

"Next is the EEG. They put a bunch of electrodes on his scalp and record his brain's rhythms. You know, you can come in to see the doctors with me if you'd like."

"Okay."

There was a knock at the door.

"Hi. I'm Carla. I'll be doing the EEG. I was told about the episode that just happened. Is he alert yet?"

"Philly?" called Angelina.

"Huh?"

"He's just starting to come around."

"Let's wait a little while," Carla said. "We'd prefer to have him wide awake for the exam. We ask him to open and close his eyes, and we flash lights—that kind of thing."

After the EEG and a bit more blood work, they were sent to make an appointment with Dr. Carter.

It had been a long day. Between Jeremy's accusations and Philly's seizure, Angelina was simply wiped out.

She got dinner ready, read to Philly, helped Aunt Rose dress for bed and left Alex watching television as she started to grade a set of papers.

She got halfway through and called it a night.

Once Angelina was in bed, her thoughts wandered back to the events of the day. "Was everything about you a lie?" Jeremy had asked. He knew nothing of her life but had the nerve to fling accusations. Angelina squeezed her eyes shut, and tears fell to her pillow.

Chapter 12

"This was called for two hours ago. Why is it still sitting on my desk?"

Jeremy swung the papers at Evelyn, his assistant, and turned to stride from the room.

"Those were faxed almost two hours ago, Dr. Bell," said Evelyn, stopping him. "I'll keep these to send over the hard copies."

"I'm sorry, Evelyn. I've been out of sorts."

Evelyn was a small woman, but she knew how to control a dynamic situation. Always competent and professional, she was Jeremy's right arm at work and a valued colleague.

She turned to him now and spoke quietly, evenly, as if she knew she was treading on thin ice. "You have been. Anything you need to talk about?"

"It will pass. Again, I'm sorry."

Back in his office, Jeremy sat down and opened a bottle of water. It was because of her—Safire, Angelina, whatever her name was.

She'd stepped back into his life earlier that week. Only she came with her son and her partner, parading about as if none of her lies had any consequences.

No wonder she had been so reluctant to get involved on the cruise. She had a son she'd lied about not having, which meant she had a relationship she'd said she hadn't had, and she had a lover—and a young one at that. He was probably already in the picture if he was doing stuff like going to her son's medical appointments.

No wonder she had seemed hesitant, and no wonder she had turned him down again when he had gone looking for her. She had probably been looking for a way to get out of it.

Regardless, he hated that he'd let his temper get in the way of doing his work. He had grilled her about her lies—or tried to—when she was clearly concerned for the health of her son. That wasn't like him. The last couple of days hadn't been like him, either. He'd been moody with his staff and his friends. He'd been difficult to get along with in general.

He knew she was having a hard time. He'd seen the tears welling up in her eyes when she was in his office being confronted with her lies. And he'd seen the tears falling when Phillip had the seizure. And her young man wasn't much support; rather, she seemed to be comforting him.

The problem was that the tears in her eyes almost broke his heart. He wanted to take her in his arms and comfort her. Instead, he was the one making her cry, and he wasn't the one who could do anything for Phillip when the seizure happened. He wasn't that kind of doctor.

The truth was that he was disappointed. He wouldn't be this angry if he hadn't really wanted things to work out between them. He wouldn't have tried to confront her if it hadn't actually mattered to him. He wouldn't have been crabby with his staff if he wasn't let down, and he wouldn't be let down if he hadn't really liked her, if he hadn't started falling for her.

And on top of that, he was supposed to be going out that evening. He was of a mind to cancel, but he'd cancelled out on the last couple of plans. Then, too, Michelle would be there, and he hadn't seen her in a little while. She was one of his best and longest friends, and he hadn't yet let her in on what had been going on with him. Her sage advice might be just what he needed, and she always lifted his spirits. He also needed to plead Rudy's case, if Rudy had a case.

He decided to make up his mind later, but then it got

busy, and he let it slide. By the time he thought about it again, it was too late. He was stuck with going out that night.

When he got down to the hospital's main lobby at six, Alistair and Reggie were already there. He hugged them both and took a seat next to Reggie, wrapping an arm around the back of Reggie's chair to talk to Alistair, who was on Reggie's other side.

"Hey, you guys. I'm not sure I'm up for tonight."

"Aren't you worried," Reggie said, nodding to the arm behind him, "that your colleagues will think you're gay?"

"No. Maybe if they do, the nurses will stop hitting on me."

Alistair laughed, knowing that the nurses did hit on him.

"Why aren't you up for tonight?" Reggie asked.

"Long day."

"And lonely night," Alistair said. "I take it that it didn't go well with Safire?"

"Actually, Angelina, and no. I saw her at her office, and then she brought the son I didn't know she had here, along with her nonexistent partner."

"Ouch," Alistair said. "She's a player?"

Except she wasn't, was she? Everything he knew about her said that she wasn't. But what he'd seen earlier that week and today said that she must be. He shrugged.

Alistair knew his moods and let it go. Reggie didn't know him as well.

"If she is, then it's better to find out now than to wait and find out later."

He shrugged again, hoping that Reggie would get the signal.

"No, trust me. It is."

Jeremy shifted in his chair, removing his arm from the back of Reggie's chair. It was replaced immediately by Alistair's arm from the other side, and he saw from the corner of his eye that Alistair was giving Reggie the signal to shut up—the neck chopping sign.

At least that made him chuckle.

"My bad. I'm sorry."

"Don't be. I'm just in a foul mood. I should have cancelled."

"Hey," Alistair said. "You don't stay away from your friends when you need them most."

"Okay. I got you."

Only they'd spoken too soon. In came Myron and Rudy, joshing each other over something and laughing.

"You're both in a good mood," Alistair said.

"I won my case today. I deserve to be in good mood," Myron said. "And this one is always in a good mood. Who's not?"

They all looked at Jeremy.

"Still pining over the one who got away?" Rudy punched him lightly on the shoulder.

"As if you had nothing to do with that." Jeremy said it with a warning in his voice—a warning for Rudy to back off.

Rudy got the message and threw his hands up. "I get you. I'm sorry."

Myron and Rudy sat down, quiet and apologetic. Jeremy realized he was being snippy again.

"Never mind. It probably wasn't you at all. She just wanted an out."

There was a question in Myron's face, but he knew better than to ask it. Alistair, wanting to prevent just that, turned the spotlight on Myron.

"What about you and what's-her-name?"

"Verniece is her name, and we're still doing okay. It's hard to have a long-distance relationship, though."

"Where is she?" Reggie asked.

"Charleston, South Carolina. It's a ten-hour drive. I'm going up for President's Day weekend."

"Is that really going to work out?" Reggie asked.

"I like her enough to try."

When Jeremy saw Michelle walk in with her friend Lynn, he stood. Their dinner group was assembled, and they were headed to a place in Coconut Grove called Berrie's for happy hour and dinner. Then they were headed to a jazz club near CocoWalk.

Michelle had dressed for the occasion. She was medium height and wore a red evening gown with black pumps. She scoffed almost imperceptibly at Myron and Rudy, but when she looked at him, her face fanned into the soft smile to which Jeremy had grown accustomed—that of someone who was like a baby sister to him. Her round face widened, and her almond-shaped eyes filled with mirth.

Lynn he didn't know, but she was equally decked out for the evening in a navy pantsuit and paisley wrap. She was taller than Michelle and lighter in color and had more elongated features. Her face remained more formal, but then, she didn't know them yet.

Berric's was packed, and laughter erupted from various tables throughout the night. Jeremy had never seen it so busy. It must have been good for business, but it wasn't as easy to have a conversation.

Dinner was uneventful, except that Rudy kept hitting on Michelle, while Michelle kept trying to deflect his attention to her friend Lynn.

When the women went to the restroom, Jeremy turned to Rudy.

"You know she's trying to get you to ask Lynn out, right?"

"What?"

"I think everyone can see that," Alistair said.

"No," Rudy said, "I didn't get that. I'm trying to get with Michelle."

"Reality check," Reggie said and snapped his fingers. "Michelle is interested in pawning you off on Lynn."

"Oh, man."

"What's wrong with Lynn?" Jeremy asked.

"Nothing's wrong with her. I'm just interested in Michelle."

"Well, for now," Alistair said, "you better play it cool and stop ignoring Lynn in favor of Michelle."

"I can do that."

Myron patted Rudy on the back. "You are clueless, aren't you?"

The guys cracked up, except for Jeremy, who wasn't in a laughing mood.

"And just so you know," Reggie added, "your jokes don't work on Michelle. Try something else."

The guys laughed again.

Next they headed to their cars and to the jazz club. It had low rotating lights and cushioned seating around the walls, with chest-high tables in the center of the room surrounding a dance floor. Jeremy danced with Michelle for a bit, while Rudy and Myron took turns with Lynn. Alistair and Reggie hung back at the table.

"Next time," Alistair said, when they had gathered again at the table, "we go to a gay bar. Heteros can have fun at a gay bar, but the reverse isn't true."

"Deal," Jeremy said.

"I don't know about going to a gay bar," Myron said.

"What have you got to lose?" Michelle said.

"His hetero virginity," Reggie said.

The rest of the table laughed. Jeremy hailed a waitress, and they ordered their last round of drinks.

"It's a little early," Jeremy said, "but I'm heading home after this. I've had a week."

Michelle butted her shoulder against his and leaned her head toward him to shout above the music. "We should talk, Bluebird. It's been a while."

"What are you doing now?"

"Let me make sure Lynn can get home, and I'll tell you."

After she shifted back from her conversation with Lynn, Michelle said, "Where are we going?"

Jeremy could feel Rudy's eyes on them, and his jealousy was palpable, but that's the way it was with him and Michelle. Anyone who came into their lives had to get used to it. It was the same with him and Alistair. He'd lost friends over his bond with Alistair, especially his sports buddies from college, but that was just the way it had to be.

"A café? A diner?"

"Oh, a diner sounds good. I'm hungry again."

Jeremy tickled his friend's ribs. Where do you put it all? You're still a toothpick."

The group separated at about eleven, and he and Michelle trailed each other to a diner that was close to her house. He wasn't hungry, but he ordered a milkshake.

Like Alistair, Michelle had visited him in Miami after he had gotten his job there. They had all fallen in love with the culture of the city, but in a way, they had also all moved to stay close to one another.

"So tell me. A little birdie said it was about a woman."

"A little birdie named Alistair, no doubt."

Michelle swallowed a bite of her burger. "Don't be mad. He would only tell me."

"I know. But before we get to that, I have to know this. Does Rudy stand a chance with you?"

"No. Rudy needs to grow up. For his age, he's the most juvenile man I've met."

"That is actually truer than you know, but still…"

"No." Michelle's hand went to her hip, and her finger went up in lecture mode. "I know he's your friend, but the day I will go out with that fool will be the day it snows in Miami."

"Okay, okay. I was just checking. I know how Rudy can be, and I can't say I blame you. Anyone else on the horizon? What about that guy from the art gallery?"

"No, that was fun while it lasted, but it didn't turn into anything. I'll let you know when something clicks. Which brings us to you."

Jeremy took a deep breath. "I told you briefly about the woman I met on the cruise."

"Safire."

"Well, her name turns out to be Angelina. Safire is her sister. She took her sister's place on the cruise."

"What happened?"

"I don't know if I want to get into the long version right now."

"Give me the short one."

He felt silly actually saying it. It showed how enormously duped he had been. "She has a son and a partner."

"Oh, no." Michelle reached her hand across the table and gave his arm a short squeeze. "Maybe it wasn't meant to be. Don't let it get you down. You have no idea how hot you are. You'll know when it's the right one."

"So you think I'm hot?"

Michelle laughed and jabbed his shoulder with her fingers.

"You know you are. It's only a matter of time."

"You're beautiful, too. How come we never hooked up?"

"I don't know. You've always been more of a brother to me."

Jeremy had barely touched his milkshake. He slid it across the table and watched Michelle's eyes light up.

"Thank you for being my sister," he said.

"Any time."

Jeremy was still drained from the week. He followed

Michelle home to make sure she got in safely and then he headed home himself. He had one more day of work for the week, and then he could rest over the weekend.

The next morning, the phone in his office buzzed. It was Evelyn.

"Dr. Bell, Dr. Carter's just left a message. He's hoping you have the results for the woman he referred on Tuesday who came in with her brother. She's scheduled for a follow-up appointment with him today. Let me get her name. Lewis. The patient's name was Phillip Lewis."

"Brother?"

"Yes, you remember. She had her cousin with her in the waiting room, and he had a seizure before—"

"Cousin?"

"Well, we got to chatting while I prepped him for the MRI."

"I should have the chart here. Let me call you back."

Jeremy had done the examination and had written the report, but he hadn't looked at details on the chart.

He flipped to the insurance papers. They only said "dependent." He turned to the release forms. Under next of kin for Phillip, it read Angelina Lewis, sister. Copies of the papers showing that she was his legal guardian were right after that.

He recalled that she'd vaguely mentioned family obligations on the cruise. Clearly, one of them was her brother, Phillip. He had simply assumed from the vast majority of his experience that the child was her son. And if Evelyn was right, which she doubtless was, the young man with her was a cousin, probably another family obligation.

Jeremy shook his head as the magnitude of his mistake dawned on him. He wondered briefly why she hadn't simply corrected him, but then he hadn't really given her a chance. He'd just dropped accusations while she was busy trying to find out about her brother's health.

It explained a lot. He'd only seen her twice since the cruise, but he'd noticed how different she was now. She walked harder. She didn't smile. He'd thought it was just her way of blowing him off, but it wasn't, or it wasn't only that. It was her march through the obligations of her life.

It explained some of the differences between her and Safire. She was the oldest, so the obligations fell on her. She set the example, so she couldn't be as free. She hadn't had the time to be free; it really was new to her. That's why she had hesitated.

What had he done?

He knew. He had made it harder, accusing her of being a liar and a cheat.

He wondered if the Angelina he had met on the cruise could survive on land, and he wanted to show her that she could. That she could take care of her family but take care of herself, too, that she could do all that she had to do and still be his "Safire."

He flipped the chart to her address and wrote it down, along with the number of her landline. She lived across town in North Miami, just as she'd said. He didn't know what he would do, but he had to do something.

Chapter 13

Angelina had let her last class go ten minutes early and had cancelled her office hours so that she could take Philly to his follow-up appointment with Dr. Carter at Miami Children's Hospital. Luckily, they'd been able to get a time for late in the afternoon. Alex had picked him up from school early and brought him to campus, and they made it across town just in time.

She had refused to give Dr. Jeremy Bell another thought, but now, walking into the building where he worked, she felt self-conscious; he could be around any corner. She didn't know how to spare herself any additional humiliation if they ran into each other, so she wanted to avoid that at all costs. But the most important thing was finding out what was wrong with Philly, so there was no avoiding the hospital itself.

She got to the neurology clinic without incident and signed Philly in.

"Good afternoon, Ms. Lewis. Dr. Carter is running about a half an hour behind right now, so it will be a little wait."

"That's no problem."

She should calm down. In reality, there was little chance of her running into Jeremy in such a big hospital.

She hadn't eaten all day and turned to the boys. "I'm going to get a cup of coffee or something. Would you guys like anything?"

"Not me," Alex said. "I just had lunch before we left."

"What about you, little one?"

Philly shook his head and continued to play with the game she'd brought him back from the cruise. He was sitting on Alex's lap, and Alex was helping him. It seemed as if they'd be all right for a little while, and the cantina was right down the hall. She stood up and headed in the direction from which they had just come.

She got some coffee and a muffin for herself and M&M's for the boys.

Just as she came out of the cantina, there he was, coming from the neurology department. He had on his lab coat and looked like the handsome doctor he was—the one that the nurses probably gawked over, the one who was out of her league. And so be it. He had used her like a harlot and then called her a liar, and that was enough. If only she could calm the flutter in her stomach.

She was too far into the hall to retreat into the cantina. She couldn't turn around without making herself even more visible. She looked around quickly for a place to hide, found a nearby door marked Utility Closet, and ducked in, hoping that he hadn't seen her.

Inside, there were racks of sheets and gowns and towels—things like that. She stood in the corner with her hand pressed to her chest feeling like an idiot and wondering what would happen if she were caught in there. Would it be better to be caught by him or by a member of the hospital staff? She couldn't exactly explain that she was hiding from a radiologist.

She waited a little while, trying to calm her breathing, and then she exhaled. By now the coast might be clear. When she turned around, however, she found a pair of brown eyes staring at her. It startled her so much, she nearly dropped her coffee. He was standing inside the door just looking at her.

"Here." He took the cup from her hand before she dropped it.

"I didn't know you were there."

"I— I came in behind you. I was looking for you to talk to you. You have every right to hide from me. I was…an idiot the last time you were here. I'm sorry."

Her hand was still across her chest, pressed above her heart. She clutched her purse close to her ribs and stepped to the side, hoping he would let her pass. He didn't.

"Angelina, I'm sorry for those things I said. Why didn't you tell me that Phillip wasn't your son and that the other young man was your cousin? You could have clarified everything."

"For all practical purposes, Philly is my son. And you already had your mind made up. Besides, it doesn't matter what you think. It only matters that Philly gets well. Now, I have to go."

In the close confines of the small room, Jeremy took a step toward her. She was almost against the wall.

"I shouldn't have said anything at all, but when I did, why didn't you just correct me? I made a fool of myself and said things that I never should have said. I shouldn't have said anything while you were worried about Phillip. I'm sorry."

"Again, it doesn't matter what you think."

He stared at her so intently that she brought her hand up to her neck. She felt naked and recalled how many times he has seen her without clothes on. She swallowed hard and took a breath.

"I don't want to put you on edge, Angelina. I want to put you at ease. I want to help. I want to know you again."

"You're no knight in shining armor. Those exist in fairy tales and on fantasy islands. You were horrible to me on Tuesday. Now, leave me alone."

"I can't leave you alone. I think about you all the time.

I was so angry because I thought that you'd lied to me—about everything, not just your name. I was stupid and presumptuous, but I want to apologize. I want to be there for you."

She had stepped back as far as she could go, so she gritted her teeth and stood her ground.

"I don't need you to be there for me. All I need is for you to do your job and tell me what's wrong with my brother."

"Don't you have any feelings for me, Angelina?"

"No."

"I don't believe you." Jeremy put the coffee cup on one of the shelves and took the final step toward her. "I don't believe you at all."

He put his arm around her and tipped his head down, bringing his lips against hers. Her body stilled, and she tensed up, aware of how inappropriate this was.

He removed her hand from across her throat and pulled her chest against his.

"Don't you remember me, Angelina?"

He brought his lips to hers again, harder this time, more insistent. Against her will, she felt her mouth parting beneath his and then felt his tongue move inside. She put her hands against his shoulders to push him away, but her hands didn't do what she said. They pressed against his shoulders and stayed there.

His arms tightened around her, and his palm came to rest against the small of her back, bringing her against his body. Her own body seemed to remember this and of its own volition pressed back against his. His lips opened hers wider, and his tongue reached farther into her mouth, sending a tingle up her spine and down to her center. Under his touch, her body started to throb.

When one of his hands found her breast, she had to choke off the whimper that tried to escape her throat, and she realized what she was doing. She tried to pull away, but his arms still claimed her body and his lips still claimed her.

He broke the kiss and put his head next to hers, breathing heavily. "Don't you remember me, Angelina? Don't you feel anything?"

His lips against her earlobe and his deep voice in her ear sent a quiver through her body, and her hips tilted involuntarily. When his arms came farther around her, encircling her, she gave up fighting and clung to his neck.

With the security of his arms surrounding her, all the fear that she'd been feeling over Philly came to the surface, and all the shame she'd felt over how her time with Jeremy had ended flooded back to her. Without forewarning, tears burst from her eyes, and her shoulders started to shake.

"It's okay, Ang. It'll be okay. Philly will be fine, and so will we."

She mustered her strength and pushed him back.

"No, we won't," she said, wiping the tears from her eyes. "First your friends get their jollies from painting me as a trollop, and then you treat me like a liar and a whore. It will never be the way it was. Just—" she sucked in a sob "—leave me alone."

She gritted her teeth and pushed passed him.

"Angelina."

She headed down the hall, wiping her eyes on the cuff of her sleeve. She didn't know what had gotten into her, just that whatever had been building up inside got free and got out and made her act ridiculous, clinging to the man who had made her feel like a fool just days before.

When she got to Philly and Alex she sat down and opened her purse, pulling out the M&M's she'd gotten for them. She didn't feel like eating anymore. And she knew that Jeremy would follow her. She had to get ready to undo the mixed signals she had just sent and find a way to do it without alerting Philly and Alex to what was going on.

As she expected, he followed. He sauntered up to them in his lab coat with her coffee in his hand.

"You forgot this," he said, taking a seat next to her.

She took the coffee without saying thank you and hoped that he would go. Instead, he leaned forward, placing his elbows on his knees, and began a relaxed conversation with the boys.

"How are you today, Phillip?"

"Fine, thank you," he said from Alex's lap, looking up from the game.

"Do you remember me? I'm Dr. Bell. I did your MRI this week."

Philly nodded. "You told me to hold still."

"I also remember you from Tuesday," he said, reaching out his hand to Alex.

Alex shook his hand. "Hi, I'm Alex, his cousin. Do you know what's wrong with him?"

"Not yet, but we're working on it. Dr. Carter is one of the best pediatric neurologists in the country, so you're in good hands."

He reached across Angelina's lap and rubbed Philly's head.

"Have you had any more seizures?"

Philly shook his head no.

"Not since Tuesday," Alex said.

"That's good. They're frightening, aren't they?"

Philly and Alex had stopped playing the game to talk with Jeremy, and Philly now scooted from Alex's lap to her own.

"Are you my doctor?"

"I'm your radiologist. I do some of your tests. Dr. Carter is your doctor. He'll decide what treatment to pursue."

Philly looked up at her. "Angie, am I going to be okay?"

It just about broke her heart. "Oh, honey, you're going to be just fine. You'll see."

She took the M&M's and tore the package for him, dumping some into his hands. She was waiting for Jeremy to leave, but he sat back next to her, resting his ankle on his knee.

"Can I get you guys anything—something to eat, maybe?"

"No, we're fine," Alex said. He was clearly interested in this older man, someone in a position of authority when it came to his cousin's illness. "Are you here to give Philly more tests?" he asked.

"No, just for support. Angelina is important to me."

"You know him, Angelina?"

She didn't know what to say. She certainly didn't want to start explaining her cruise to her younger cousin. She smiled weakly and nodded.

"So you're a doctor, and you do X-rays? I didn't know that doctors did X-rays."

"Not all people who do X-rays are doctors. There are also technicians. But some doctors are specially trained to interpret the results of the various X-rays and scans. We're radiologists. I specialize in brain scans, so I'm a neuroradiologist."

Alex was clearly intrigued by the presence of a Black man who'd made something of his life, who was at ease in the world.

"How long did it take you to become one?"

"A long time—undergraduate degree, medical school, specialization. I haven't been practicing on my own for that long, but it was worth it. What do you do?"

Angelina saw Alex's face close and his head drop. The question was a sore spot for him, she knew, but she hadn't known how to prevent it.

"Nothing right now. I haven't made up my mind yet."

"It'll come to you. There's this bracelet that I've seen

that says 'All that wander are not lost.' Sometimes we have to wander a little bit to find our way."

"Did—"

"Phillip Lewis," the receptionist called.

They all stood.

Jeremy rubbed Philly's head. "Okay, little one." He shook Alex's hand again. "It was nice to meet you this time." Then he looked beyond Philly to Angelina. His eyes bored into her, and she almost looked away. "You let me know how things go. I'll see you again soon."

She didn't know what to do. She adjusted Philly on her hip, nodded briefly and turned to follow the receptionist. This was not what she'd meant when she said for him to leave her alone, but she would have to wait to make that point.

Dr. Carter said what Jeremy had indicated. They didn't know yet what was wrong with Philly; all of the tests they had done were inconclusive.

"In a lot of cases, the cause of seizures remains unknown," Dr. Carter said.

"Isn't there another test you can do? I read about a CT scan."

"The MRI gives us the same kind of information, but it tells us more. We choose it over the CT scan whenever possible."

"There was a PET scan and something else."

"The SPECT is the other one. We use those once we've identified areas that we are considering for surgery. We're not anywhere near there. Because these are the first seizures that he's had, what I want to do is monitor him for a month without medication. If the seizures continue, we'll start him on a low dose of anticonvulsants."

"He's had three. Shouldn't we do that now?"

"I want to wait for two reasons. We need to determine the frequency of the seizures to estimate the correct dosage to use, and such medications have side effects, so if they're not needed we don't want to use them.

"Trust me here, and let me see you again in one month. In the meantime, I want you to keep a journal of any seizures that occur. Watch him closely, and time the seizures."

They talked more, and in the end, she knew what to do if Philly had another seizure and when to take him to the E.R.

When she got home that evening her nerves were shot from the stress of the day, but she got dinner ready and kept Aunt Rose company for a little while. At nine-thirty, when she was trying to grade papers, she got a conference call from two of her friends—Gloria and Amelia—who were trying to get her to go out on Friday night.

"No, I can't. Besides papers to grade, my brother has started having seizures, and I need to stay close to home."

"I'm so sorry to hear that," Amelia said. "Look, you can't wait until we call to fill us in."

"I know, but once the semester gets going…"

"No more excuses," Gloria chimed in. "We're having lunch next week."

"Maybe not," Angelina said. "My great-aunt has a doctor's appointment for her arthritis on Thursday."

"Girl, you're doing too much," Amelia said.

"I know. It will get better when the semester is over."

When she got off the phone, she turned back to her papers, but grading made her think about Alex. It was endearing to see Alex's admiration for an older man, to see him trying to figure out how to find his way. She wanted him to go to school, but he didn't seem to be taking her suggestion seriously. And he didn't seem to be looking hard for a job, either.

Of course, he'd been very helpful with Philly, and he was getting to be more helpful with Aunt Rose. She wanted him to be okay, too. She was going to bring up school again.

That left her having to figure out how to set Jeremy straight.

She turned back to her papers. She was distracting herself when she needed to catch up. She would deal with that later.

Chapter 14

Jeremy put down the bowl of nachos and crossed his ankles on the coffee table. It had been a few days since he'd seen Angelina, and no reconciliation was on the horizon, but he had started to hope. For now, that was enough. His spirits were good enough to have his friends over for a game, and he didn't even have to cook.

"Honey," Alistair yelled from right next to him, "do you need any help?"

Reggie's head appeared in the doorway leading to the kitchen. "No, I'm fine. Hey, Jeremy, where's your strainer?"

"Under the sink to the right."

"Game started yet?" Reggie asked.

"Nope," Alistair said.

"Then come open these jars."

Alistair swung his head in a large circle and then scooted to the edge of the couch, continuing to watch the pre-game coverage.

"You know," Myron said, "for a gay guy, you're such a typical male."

"You know," Alistair responded, "if I wasn't a typical male, I wouldn't be a gay guy."

Jeremy chuckled.

"I'll be back."

When Alistair got inside the kitchen, they heard Reggie peal with laughter and then go silent.

"At least somebody's getting a little something," said Myron.

"Are you all scandalizing Michelle?" Jeremy called toward the kitchen.

Michelle came into the living room wearing sweatpants and a sweatshirt with her team's logo. She put a bowl of chips and dip on the coffee table and took a seat on the couch. She had been staying in more regular contact with Jeremy since their talk, and he knew she was making sure that he was all right.

"It'll take more than that to scandalize me."

Jeremy drew Michelle's head onto his shoulder, and at that moment, he wished she was Angelina.

"You ready for the game?" he asked.

"Yep."

"You're in a better mood," Myron commented to Jeremy. "Anything we should know?"

"No, not really."

Alistair came back and took a seat.

"Not really means a little bit," Alistair said. "Spill."

"Well, I found out that Angelina's not involved and doesn't have a son. But she still doesn't want to see me."

"So, who was the boy?" Michelle asked.

"It appears she's raising her little brother and helping out her cousin."

"Dag," Alistair said. "How old is the brother?"

"He's six."

"That sounds like an awful lot of responsibility—too much," Myron said.

It wasn't something Jeremy had really considered before, but he was considering it now. What would it mean to have a six-year-old son at his age?

"I think it's admirable of her," Michelle said.

"Of course you would," Myron said. "I do, too. I'm just thinking about getting into a relationship with someone who, for all practical purposes, has a six-year-old child."

"So you're saying she comes with too much baggage?" Alistair asked, not buying it.

"I'm just saying think about it. That's all. You can't play with being a father."

"You know, with her, I don't think I'd mind the responsibility. But I am a few years older than you."

"Age is not the issue."

"Well, in a way it is. Look at it this way. We were still in school when a lot of our peers were getting married and having children. It changed our perception of when those things should happen. My parents had me by the time they were my age."

"And mine had me by now, too," Michelle said.

"I get it," Myron said. "I'm just saying to make sure you really want this woman before getting in with her kid."

"I will do that."

"Okay. That's all."

"Not that it's actually an option," Jeremy said, remembering. "I think her last words to me were 'Leave me alone.'"

The group laughed and then apologized.

"It's okay. It's actually rather funny."

"You are in a better mood," Alistair said.

"You know," Michelle said, "that's never stopped you before. What about now?"

"I haven't given up yet. I'll let you know."

"Is the game on yet?" Reggie called from the kitchen.

"No," they all called back.

"Then come do some mixing."

Alistair swung his head in a circle again and stood up.

"Okay," Jeremy said. "Now he just wants to play."

They all laughed.

Alistair headed to the kitchen. "And what my baby wants…"

They heard Reggie give a screeching laugh and then go quiet.

They all cracked up.

A week later, Jeremy found himself acting on what he had said—he hadn't given up yet. With the address from her medical file in his pocket, he was on his way across town. He was halfway there when it occurred to him that he shouldn't show up empty-handed.

He saw a bakery first, so he got the trio an assortment of pastries. He also stopped into a department store to get a token for Angelina, and he needed a card to go with it, so he found a drug store.

He knew he'd found the address when he recognized Phillip playing in the front yard. He had on jeans and a baseball shirt and was playing ball with some other children. Jeremy was glad to see Phillip having a good time, but he didn't know what the reception would be inside. That, however, wouldn't stop him from trying.

"Hey, Phillip."

The boy got hold of the ball he was playing with, passed it along to one of the other children and ran up to him.

"Hi, Dr. Bell."

"You remember my name. You're a smart one, aren't you? You can call me Jeremy, though."

"Jeremy."

"Is your sister around?"

"She's in the kitchen."

Jeremy looked at the box in his hand. "Would she let you have a pastry?"

"Uh-huh."

Jeremy opened the box and let Phillip pick out a confection.

"Have you had any more seizures recently?"

Phillips shook his head.

"Excellent. You want to walk me up to the house?"

"Okay."

Phillip let him in the front door, which opened into the living room. The furniture was stately but well used and a bit dated. The house looked as though it had been lived in for a long time but by a loving family.

On the walls there was floral wallpaper that was now somewhat faded, and the sofa set was covered with an old tapestry, probably to hide the need for reupholstering. The wooden coffee table in the center of the room had scuffs from use and white spots from hot plates. The stereo was antique, and the shelves of the entertainment center sagged in the middle where there had been heavy loads. The carpet, another floral design, was worn along the walking path. The flat-screen television and wireless telephone stood out as new among the old.

Beyond the age of things, though, the room told the history of a loving family. Family photographs lined the credenza. Memorabilia that was probably older than he was filled a china cabinet. Handmade doilies covered the arms of the sofas and tops of the end tables. Records and books and knickknacks filled the entertainment center around the television. Everything was scrubbed, polished, dusted, and loved—nicks and chips and fading and all.

Alex was on the sofa and straightened when he saw that there was company.

"Hi, Alex," Jeremy said.

"Hello."

He shook the young man's hand and offered him a pastry.

"I'm looking for Angelina. Phillip said she's in the kitchen."

"Yes, she is." He didn't get up from the couch but called out to her. "Angelina, you have company."

Jeremy couldn't help but smile, glad as he was that he

would be seeing Angelina again and getting a glimpse of her in her own space, her home.

Angelina appeared in the kitchen doorway and let out a heavy sigh when she saw that it was Jeremy. Her momentary surprise faded to a haggard look—one that he longed to soothe out of her features with gentle kisses. Without a word, she turned around and walked back into the kitchen. A bit worried that she had dismissed him completely, Jeremy frowned and followed her.

He found her standing behind an elderly woman who was sitting at the dining table. The older woman's hair was damp, and there was a towel tucked into the neck of her floral dress. Angelina had a comb and a jar of pomade and had made one braid so far. She continued to part the woman's hair and grease her scalp, ignoring him.

"Good afternoon, ma'am. I'm Jeremy, a friend of Angelina's."

"Afternoon."

"Can I offer you a pastry?" He opened the box for her.

"Let me try that one." She pointed to one.

He looked around for a napkin, found one on the table and handed the woman the sweet roll.

"Angelina? Where's your manners? Introduce me to the young man."

"Jeremy, this is my great-aunt, Aunt Rose."

"Pleased to meet you," Aunt Rose said.

"Aunt Rose, this is Jeremy Bell. He's a radiologist at Miami Children's Hospital, where they're treating Philly."

"I see. You got any news on what's wrong with the boy?"

"No, I don't. We're still looking into it, though. He's in good hands."

"I hope they find out soon. Them spells he gets are enough to scare the living daylights out of you."

"I know. I saw one myself."

Since Angelina wasn't joining in the conversation, he decided to talk to the aunt.

"How are you doing?"

"I have better days and worse days. But I'm eighty-four years old."

"Eighty-four," Jeremy echoed. "Congratulations."

"Ain't me. Thank the good Lord."

"Well, you must have good genes."

The old woman smiled at that. Then she felt for Angelina's hand in her hair and tapped it.

"This ain't how we taught you. Offer the young man some iced tea."

Angelina sighed, clearly rattled to be impeded in her progress with the hair.

"Can I get you some iced tea, Jeremy?"

"Sure. Thank you."

She got two glasses and poured the last of the iced tea for her great-aunt and Jeremy.

Jeremy sipped his drink and got comfortable. The kitchen was like the living room. It was a used house, but there was love in it.

"What did you do before you retired, Aunt Rose?"

"What? Well, I did more than one thing."

While her great-aunt was telling the story of her work life, Angelina greased and braided her hair, never looking at him. When a buzzer went off, she washed her hands, moved clothes from the washer to the dryer and came back to her great-aunt's hair.

She was wearing sweat pants, and a T-shirt and sneakers, and her hair was pulled back in a ponytail. She looked comfortable, but she was also beautiful. The T-shirt was loose, but it didn't conceal the gentle swell of her bosom, and the sweatpants hugged the curves of her rear and her thighs. He could remember the feel of her firm rump in his palms as he pressed her body against his. Jeremy stopped himself and pulled his mind from the gutter.

He could see that her family obligations didn't end with Phillip and Alex. She was worked to the bone. He saw how tired she was in the soft circles under her eyes and the resignation etched into her jaw. His smiling Angelina was nowhere to be found, and he wondered if he would ever have her back. As soon as she would let him, he would be getting her some help around here.

When Angelina was finished, she moved her great-aunt into the living room. Then she came back to dismiss him.

"I don't have very long. I have to get ready for classes tomorrow. Why are you here?"

"I came to see you."

She piled the hair supplies into the towel and placed it on the counter. Then she got out some chicken parts from the fridge and started to wash and skin them.

"Have you seen enough?"

"No, I haven't."

"You need to leave anyway."

"Let me help you with dinner. I make pretty good—"

She turned to him. "This is not going to work, Jeremy. Let it go."

"I think it can work, and I can't let it go. I'm so sorry for the things I said to you in my office, for the things I thought. I'm sorry for the things my friends said. They're not bad people, but they have a little growing up to do. And by the way, Alistair wasn't participating. Give me another chance. Give us another chance. Go out with me next weekend."

"No. Look. This isn't a fantasy, and you're sure as hell no prince charming. I have a family to take care of. I'm not the person you met on that cruise, and you're not the person I met, either. I don't have the time or energy to make an even bigger fool of myself than I have already."

"I am the person you met. I just make mistakes sometimes, like us regular mortals do. Everyone is not a super-woman like you. And you don't have to do it all alone. Let me be there for you."

Angelina crossed to the cupboard and took out a box of pasta.

"It's not about whether I do things alone or not. It's about what happened between us and what ended that and what's happened since then. You know, probably the only reason you're here now is because no one ever tells you no. You're handsome and charming and financially comfortable. You can have whomever you want. Well, go find them, and leave me alone."

"The person I want is standing right here. And I've been told no. Not a lot, I'll admit, but I'm not spoiled. And I can tell that you don't have a lot of time. I'm not here to make things harder. I want to make things easier."

"Make them easier by leaving me alone."

Jeremy got up from his seat and leaned against the counter.

"You know what I think? I think you're afraid. You're afraid to want me, afraid to let yourself rely on someone else a little, afraid what people might think, afraid to be the woman who's not afraid to get what she wants, as Safire so eloquently put it. Speaking of which, where is your sister? How come she's not helping out with all of this? You have Philly, who's having seizures, a great-aunt who needs round-the-clock care and a cousin who doesn't know what he wants to do with himself."

"Leave my younger sister out of it. And it's none of your business how we arrange affairs in our family. And if you think I'm afraid, go find yourself someone who isn't. Go."

"No."

He approached her, putting his hands on her shoulders. She stilled and inhaled. He started to pull her into his arms, but she pushed him off before he could wrap them around her, before he could kiss her. He knew that if he had, she would have responded, just as she had every time since the very beginning. And she clearly didn't want that. It would belie all her protestations.

He looked at her and sighed.

"Okay. I'll leave you to cooking and class prep. I'm not here to make your life harder. When you see that, maybe you'll let me in. That," he pointed to the small bag on the table next to the pastry box, "is for you. Look at it when you have a chance."

Chapter 15

"There's more to it than you've indicated in your paper," Angelina said. "By drawing upon the epic narrative tradition, Douglass is not only assuming control of Western discourse, he's using the master discourse against the masters. He's doing what Audre Lorde said couldn't be done when she said that 'the master's tools will never dismantle the master's house.'"

When she looked up to see whether or not her student was getting what she was trying to say, Angelina jumped in her seat. Jeremy had come in and was sitting quietly in the chair at the far end of her office. He had on a casual suit that showed off his athletic shape and sat with one ankle propped up on the other knee, casually taking it all in. Angelina couldn't react with a student at hand, but she would have a word or two for Dr. Bell in a moment.

"I think I understand," Annette, her student, was saying. "I need to show that Douglass is not only using the epic tradition but using it as a form of resistance."

"Yes, I think that will deepen your argument and honor the complexity of Douglass's narrative strategy. And I raised that point in lecture, so you can draw from lecture notes to boost your argument."

"Who was the critic you mentioned about the master's tools?"

"Audre, *A-U-D-R-E*, Lorde, with an *e*."

"Can I use her in my revision?"

"Yes, by all means. And don't forget to add textual evidence of Douglass's use of the epic and of the way it serves as resistance to the dominant ideology."

"Okay. Thank you, Dr. Lewis."

"I'll see you in class on Monday."

Before Angelina could stop and formulate a few choice words for Jeremy, her next student walked in and took a seat. She glared at Jeremy but decided to continue with her office hours.

"Hi, Dr. Lewis."

"Peter, right?"

The young man nodded. "I have questions about the *History of the Black Atlantic* and about my paper."

"Did you bring your paper with you?"

He pulled out his paper, and Angelina flipped through it.

"You didn't do well here. Half of what kept you back is an incomplete understanding of the text. The other half is the prose. Let's address both."

"Well, to be honest, I hadn't finished reading the book when the paper was due."

Over the student's shoulder, she saw Jeremy's shoulders shaking in silent laughter, and she got angry with him for making her want to laugh.

"That explains it. If you want the grade, you have to do the work."

"What I really need to know is what I can do to bring my score up."

"How much of our class have you missed, Peter? Honestly."

"Well, I have practice late at night, so I miss sometimes."

"Student athletes are only excused when the team is away. I asked because I don't see you all the time, and if you were in class, you'd know that you can revise the first paper and the first take-home exam."

"Can I come back to go over it?"

"You're here now."

"Yeah, but I have to see another teacher at four across campus."

"Well, I'm sorry I kept you waiting. Come back Monday afternoon. If I don't see you, I'll take it as a sign of lack of commitment."

"I'll be here, Dr. Lewis."

The next student came in and sat down.

"Hello, Dr. Lewis. I wrote about gender issues during slavery, and I didn't do well."

"Marcia. I remember your paper because I'm so interested in your topic. Take it out so that we can go over it. What you needed was more evidence to support your claim. You can't overgeneralize about circumstances for everyone based on the experience of one or two people, so you had a great deal of inaccuracy. You have to remember that both Douglass and Jacobs were, in some way, exceptions to the rules. I can give you several sources that will help you fix those inaccuracies and produce a stronger piece. Like here, where you say that women worked in the house. On plantations, most slaves, male and female, worked in the fields. Remember our reading about Sojourner Truth?"

"Yes, but if I have so many inaccuracies, maybe I don't really have an argument anymore."

"You don't. You're going to have to start by qualifying your argument and your subpoints, but I can give you some ideas on how to do that successfully."

After Marcia left, Angelina waited. No other student came in, so she finally turned to Jeremy, who smiled at her, got up and came over to take the chair she had been using with her students.

"Actually, Dr. Lewis, I didn't read the book before I did my homework."

He laughed, and she couldn't help but chuckle.

When the moment was over, though, she returned to herself.

"What are you doing here?"

"I took off early to catch you and take you to dinner, maybe do a little window shopping before that. I need to get something for my brother's birthday."

"No. I need to get dinner ready at home, and I have laundry to do, not to mention—"

"I called home. Philly is doing fine, and Alex is willing to look after both him and Aunt Rose for a few hours. He didn't even want the babysitting money I offered him."

She started to shake her head and was about to say something else, but he cut her off.

"I'll get you home in time to do laundry, and you can take a couple hours off from paper grading and prep and... whatnot. You have to eat, and we'll get some take-out for the family on the way home."

One of her colleagues, Dr. Albert Jones, poked his head in the door.

"One moment, Jeremy. Yes, Dr. Jones?"

"Sorry to interrupt. I'm wondering if you'll be able to make it to a Curriculum Committee meeting next Wednesday at three."

"Yes, I will. Can you let me know where? Oh, and I have the information on best practices that I was supposed to collect. Do you want to see it beforehand?"

"It's in Room 426, but I'll email with confirmation once I get a quorum. And just bring the information."

"Dr. Jones," Jeremy said, "help me convince Dr. Lewis to take a few hours off."

Angelina was appalled. "Never mind, Dr. Jones." She waved her hands. "It would take too long to explain."

As soon as her colleague left, Angelina glared at Jeremy. "Don't embarrass me at my place of work, or I'll have a restraining order taken out on you."

"I'm going to say that to everyone who comes in unless you say yes."

"Then let's get out of my office."

While Jeremy chuckled, she stood and started packing her books.

"This is your side of town," he said. "Where would you like to eat? And where can I look for something for my brother?"

"What do you want to get him?"

Jeremy seemed perplexed and shrugged.

"How old is he?"

"Twenty-five."

"Does he like art?"

"Not enough to have any."

"Cars?"

"Yes, actually."

"How about a GPS system for his car—one of those things that tells him where to find stuff?"

"That's a good idea. Where around here can we get one?"

"That's a good question."

They chuckled.

"Wait," Angelina said. "Let's check the internet."

They found an electronics store nearby that carried GPS navigation systems and hit the store before deciding on a restaurant. It didn't take Jeremy long to select one, and then they headed to a small, family-owned Italian restaurant that Angelina knew.

They were seated at a little table for two and offered menus.

"I already know what I want," Angelina said.

"And I'll have what she's having. I can tell from the look in her eyes that it must be good."

"It is," Angelina said.

"And do you have garlic bread?" Jeremy asked.

"Coming right up."

Angelina looked at Jeremy and shook her head. She

was here; she might as well try to enjoy it a bit. At least he wouldn't try anything with her in public.

But looking at Jeremy made her long for those days on the cruise when she could smile at him, when he would put his hand on the small of her back and make her shiver, when she could touch those firm broad shoulders and peer into those warm brown eyes. If only it hadn't all been a mistake; if only the waking fantasy she'd had was true. For a moment it flooded back—all that she'd started to feel when his fingers were intertwined with hers or when they toppled on the floor of the roller-skating rink and couldn't stop laughing or when...

His voice cut through her reverie.

"So how long have you been looking after your brother?"

"My mom had me young, but she had Philly later in life. They couldn't control her blood pressure, and she died in childbirth. That was six years ago. My father was devastated, and I was still at home. I went to school from home, so I looked after Philly a lot even then. Then my father died in a car accident two years later, and Philly became mine. And so did Aunt Rose."

Jeremy reached over and took her hand. It sent a tingle up her spine. She ignored it, yet she didn't remove her hand.

"I'm sorry to hear about your parents. Does Phillip call you Mommy?"

"Sometimes he does, usually when he's upset or sleepy or scared."

"Your sister is twenty-three. How old are you?"

"Twenty-nine. That's why Philly became mine. She was seventeen when my mother passed and nineteen when my father passed. She was still in college, and she's not really... domestic."

"Shouldn't she help out more?"

"I don't know. Maybe. She has such life, such spirit. I don't want to see that taken away."

"And your life, your spirit?"

Angelina took a breath and shook her head. There was nothing to say to that.

His fingers were caressing hers, and a shiver ran up her back. Still, she didn't pull her hand away.

"What about Alex?"

"Alex is our cousin. His branch of the family didn't fare as well as ours. He needed a place to go when his mother started dating someone a couple years back. It was a bad situation, and he's family. You take care of family. He's a good kid. He just needs to find his way, as you said."

"How about your career? Have you been able to advance at all? How can you with all these demands at home?"

"I have an article I need to get done now, and I'm behind in publishing. When I come up for tenure in a couple of years, it will be a question. Teaching and committees make it impossible to get much done during the school year, and over the summer I usually teach to make the extra money. I start something, and before it's done the school year has started again."

Angelina found herself looking down at the table setting in front of her. She hadn't really realized what a sore spot her career was for her. It was embarrassing to have to admit such deficiency.

Jeremy took her chin with his free hand, rubbing her cheek with his thumb. Even though she knew he only meant to be soothing, goose bumps ran down her back.

"Ang, you're raising a family, taking care of an elderly aunt. Cut yourself some slack. It will come."

"I know." She shook her head to rid herself of the fallen mood that had come over her and of the shivers that were still running over her spine. She took her hand back as he removed his fingers from her chin. "What about you? How old are you?"

"I'm thirty-two. Both of my parents are still alive. I

want you to meet them. And I have one brother, Edward, who's—"

"Twenty-five."

"Yes."

She set her hands back on the table, and he took one of them again, looking at it as he laced his fingers through hers, caressing them. It was a simple gesture, but it sent a thrill through Angelina's body and lit a fire in the pit of her belly. She sucked in her breath and pulled her hand away, hoping that he hadn't noticed anything.

Over dinner, they talked about her teaching and his work, her great-aunt and his parents. Near the end, he ordered two more of the lasagnas they'd had so that she could take them home for Philly and Alex, and he ordered a chicken dish for Aunt Rose, hoping it wouldn't be too spicy for her. While they waited for the take-out order, he turned the conversation toward their relationship.

"Angelina, I want to see you. Go out with me again."

"I don't really date in real life. I'm too busy with work and home. And the accusations you made show me what you really think of me. It's as bad as what your friends were joking about."

"I was angry, and I didn't know any better. Especially after finding out that you weren't who you said you were and hadn't told me. It was easy to believe that you also hadn't told me other things."

"Maybe neither of us is who we were on the cruise. I know I'm not."

"Yes, you are. You're smart and beautiful and vivacious and erotic and playful and all of that. You just won't let yourself be."

She hated it when he was sweet. It made her want to rid herself of caution when she knew she couldn't.

"Maybe it's the way I cope with a hectic life. But I can't change that, and neither can you. Let it go."

"Like I said, I can't."

She took a breath and stretched her head from side to side.

"Tired?"

"Yes, very."

"I would love to massage you to sleep."

She looked at him. He didn't seem to be getting fresh, only saying what had come to mind, but the thought sent a warm gush into the pit of her stomach, and now that they were getting ready to leave, it made her a little uncomfortable. She didn't want him to try anything, especially not with the conflicting emotions moving through her.

When the take-out order came and the check with it, he handed over a card.

"You don't have to pay. Most of this was mine."

"I have it, Angelina. Let me treat you, all of you. I'm not here to make things harder. Remember?"

She sighed and let it go, knowing that he could afford it in a way that she couldn't.

He walked her back to her car, carrying the food.

At her car he put his arms around her, pulling her into a hug. She thought he would kiss her and was ready to protest, but he didn't. He simply hugged her, said good-night and moved off to his car.

She drove home in silence, her head spinning. She was tired, but she also wished that something of her time at sea was part of her life now—some of the freedom, some of the romance, some of the choice.

She didn't really know why she had gone out with Jeremy. He hadn't actually strong-armed her. But that was part of it—wanting more than she had now.

Then she remembered the gift he'd left for her. She'd forgotten to mention it. She'd meant to tell him that he had to take it back. If not, she needed to thank him for it or to say something. It was a gold bracelet with a ship charm along with an apology card in which he'd written a sweet note.

Maybe she was just afraid.

Chapter 16

Jeremy watched the florist load the two filled vases into a bag and separate them with tissue paper, but he was thinking about Angelina—the way her body shivered when he'd caressed her fingers over the table, the way her face had leaned toward his touch when he ran his thumb along her jaw. Her body was so responsive to his touch that he'd had to control himself in the restaurant and at her car to stop from seeking more.

He took the handles of the bag and braced the bottom to keep the vases steady. The short, fat one with yellow lilies and while calla lilies was for Aunt Rose, and the tall, thin one with pink and red roses was for Angelina.

He was on his way to Angelina's on a Saturday. He wanted to see her again, and since she wouldn't invite him, he was just dropping by. He had given her a little time, trying not to crowd her. He remembered from medical school what it meant to have too much on your plate and what it was like when someone else didn't understand. He didn't want to be that person to Angelina.

Jeremy heard the television from outside the front door and rang the bell. Alex opened the door and straightened up when he saw Jeremy.

"Hello, Dr. Bell."

"Call me Jeremy."

"You're here to see Angelina? Is it Philly?"

"No new news on Philly. I'm just here to see Angelina."

"Come in," Alex said, stepping aside. "She's in the shower, but I'll let her know that you're here."

Jeremy entered the living room and found Aunt Rose in front of the television, watching an episode of *The Golden Girls*.

"Here's the young man who brought the pastry. How are you, dear? Tell me your name again."

"I'm Jeremy, Jeremy Bell, a friend of Angelina." He got her flowers out of the bag. "These are for you, Aunt Rose."

He held the flowers in front of her for her to see and then placed them on the table beside her and sat down on the couch next to her easy chair.

"When my husband and I lived down on Eastbrook," she said, "there was a flower shop in the next block. That man used to bring me flowers every other week when he got paid. These here is lilies—yellow lilies. They pretty as the ones I used to get. Thank you, son."

"How have you been keeping, ma'am?"

"Oh, it comes and goes. Nothing to talk about."

"How long ago did you lose your husband?"

Aunt Rose sat up and started calculating. "Now, let's see. That was a while ago. I was sixty-four. That was some twenty years ago now."

"I see. I'm still sorry to hear it."

"Thank you. What else is in them bags you brought?"

Jeremy wasn't expecting the question. Trying to engage Aunt Rose, he'd almost forgotten about the bags.

"I brought some flowers for Angelina, and I brought a game for Phillip and Alex."

"Flowers are always good for a lady. Where's Philly, though? Alex, go call him. We supposed to be keeping an eye out."

Alex got up from the other sofa and jogged up the steps two at a time. In a moment, Phillip came down the steps in front of him.

"Philly," Aunt Rose opened her arms for him to come. He stepped into the circle next to her legs and looked at Jeremy.

"Hi, Phillip. How are you doing? Any more seizures?" Phillip shook his head. "Hi."

"Last week there was one. Frightened us all to death." Aunt Rose squeezed Phillip in a hug. "He's been fine here lately."

"I brought something for you and Alex. I hope you don't already have one."

Jeremy pulled a PlayStation out of the bag and put it on the table. Then he pulled out some games for it and riffled through them to separate them before handing two to Phillip and two to Alex.

"You can play his," he said to Alex, "but we probably don't want him playing yours."

"This is great," Alex said. "Thank you."

"You too, Phillip," Aunt Rose said. "Thank Jeremy for the present."

"Thank you, Jeremy."

"Do you know how to hook it up?" he asked Alex.

"No, but I can figure it out."

Jeremy handed Alex the box and got up to help him read through the directions.

"Aunt Rose," said Alex, "do you mind if we use the television for a little while?"

"No, child. You all go ahead."

Once Alex and Jeremy got the game hooked up, Alex called Phillip over.

"Which one of yours do you want to put in first?"

"I like this one."

They put in the game, and Phillip and Alex took seats on the floor in front of the television to start playing. Jeremy went back to his seat near Angelina's great-aunt. When they got the game going, he explained the objective and some of the moves to her, not sure she understood. He was wrong to doubt.

"Get those things, Philly," she said after a while. "Don't worry that Alex is winning. Get 'em."

"Hey," Alex said, "you're not supposed to take sides." He laughed.

"I'm only helping him. You're winning."

"I'm supposed to win. I'm older."

"No, the little ones can win sometimes."

"Not this time," Alex said, into the game. "I got him this time."

"What's going on here?"

Jeremy turned around to see Angelina. She'd come down the steps so quietly that they hadn't noticed her. She had on her orange capris, a white chemise blouse and flat sandals on her feet. She looked beautiful, and he wanted nothing more than to take her back upstairs and peel every stitch of clothing from her newly washed body, but he knew that wouldn't happen. She put her purse down on the credenza and came into the living room.

"The children just playing this new game that Jeremy brought," Aunt Rose explained.

"We're playing this game," Philly said, moving to the television. Alex put it on pause. "You have to get around these and get these to get powers so you can get to the next level. Come look."

"In a second."

Jeremy had gotten up when he heard her voice and now stood in front of her. She didn't seem terribly pleased to see him. In fact, her expression said that he was an intrusion. But she tolerated his kiss on the forehead and took the flowers from him when he got them out of the bag.

"Thank you."

"Come see, Angie," Phillip said.

They both moved to the couch.

"Okay, go ahead," she said, and Alex started the game again.

Phillip started telling her what he was doing in the game and how it worked.

"That's very good, Philly."

"You want to try it, Angelina?" Alex asked.

"No, not this time." She got up. "Let me get some lunch ready so you guys can eat."

Jeremy followed her into the kitchen. "Can I take all of you to lunch?"

"No, we're just having sandwiches." Then she added, "You don't have to bring things for us."

"I like bringing things for you. Here, let me help with the sandwiches. I'm the sandwich master."

She stepped out of the way for him to spread the mayonnaise and started opening cans of chicken noodle soup.

"I thought we decided that this wasn't a good idea," she said.

"No, you decided. I disagreed."

"I can't play with you today. I have a million things to get done."

"Maybe I can help."

"Angelina," Aunt Rose called from the living room.

"Yes, Aunt Rose."

"Be sure to make enough for Jeremy."

"I am," she called back, getting Jeremy two more slices of bread.

"Good, dear."

"I don't need help on my errands."

"You have it anyway. Don't fight it."

She let out an exasperated breath but held her tongue.

"It's time to eat," she called. "Put the game on pause."

When everyone was finished, Angelina got up from the table.

"You guys clear the table and help Aunt Rose back to the living room. Alex, do you need anything from the store?"

"No, Angelina."

She seemed not to believe him, but she let it go.

"Do you need any other games?" Jeremy asked.

"Actually…" Alex looked at Angelina to see if she would mind.

Angelina stopped and looked at Alex on the couch. It was clear that she was taking this seriously.

"I can get it," she said. "What?"

"They have a new Madden game out."

Jeremy didn't know the games, but he certainly knew sports.

"Madden the football player?" Jeremy asked.

"Yeah, that or *Thundershock*."

"Okay," Angelina said. "We'll look."

Alex still hesitated.

"You don't have to get it, though."

"I know. I'll see," Angelina said. She picked up her keys and then turned back to the boys.

"When you're ready, play for an hour, and then let Aunt Rose watch her shows."

"Okay," Alex said, putting in the game again.

"Philly?" Angelina called.

He went to her, and she hugged him against her legs. "An hour. Is that okay?"

"Uh-huh."

"Oh," Aunt Rose remembered, "Ms. Lee gonna stop by this afternoon with some greens."

"That's good. I'll make something to go with them. I'll get something at the grocery store. See you guys soon."

She grabbed her purse from the credenza, which now had her flowers on it, and Jeremy followed her out to her car. It was clear that she was just tolerating his presence.

He went with her to the pharmacy for her great-aunt's

medicines, then to a discount store to pick up something Philly needed for school and some other household items. Then they found the games that Alex wanted.

"That's how much they cost?" Angelina asked. "Why are they so expensive?"

"It's just how they can price them. It's big business. But I'm getting these."

"Are you sure? You've already gotten them games. We don't have to get these now. I can get them for his birthday."

"Nope, this is part of my treat."

She shook her head but held her peace.

Next she stopped so she could get copies of a test she needed for Monday, then she mailed some bills. This went quickly, and the two of them were pretty quiet along the way.

"The next stop is going to take a while," she said. "Maybe I should drop you home before I go."

Jeremy reached out for her, running his fingers along the edge of her face. He saw her shoulders lift and her body shudder as she looked at him.

"I'm spending the day with you. What's next?"

"The grocery store. It's the last errand before home."

"Let's go."

They got a cart and started going up and down the aisles as she loaded it.

"So tell me," he said. "Why didn't you think Alex was telling the truth when he said he didn't need anything?"

She sighed. "Because he never says he needs anything, and he doesn't have a job, so he must need something— clothes, shoes, to go out somewhere, something."

"Do you give him an allowance?"

"Yes, until he gets a job. But it's small."

"It's good that he doesn't want to put a strain on you. You're already providing everything he needs."

"Yes, but we're his family now. He should be able to say if he wants something."

"He did today."

"Yes, that's why I let you get them. Usually, he never does."

They were in the cookie aisle. Jeremy took out his phone and hit a preprogrammed number.

"What kind of cookies do you guys like?" he asked. "Philly wants the one with the cream in the middle."

Angelina swatted him as he started loading the requests into the cart.

"Ask Aunt Rose…vanilla wafers. We got it. Is there anything else?…Okay. What kind of ice cream?…Okay. We're not there yet, but we'll get it."

"You are crazy," Angelina said.

"We like cookies."

When they got to the meat section, he added some extra selections. "These are on me."

She tried to get the lamb out of the cart but he got hold of it and turned around while she chased it. Before long, they were both laughing like children.

"This is silly," she said and swatted him again.

"But it made you laugh. I love to hear you laugh, Angelina."

She got quiet for a moment, and he wrapped his arm around her, drawing her along the meat section.

"I'm going to fix the lamb for you guys one day. Just hold it for me."

"I don't actually know how to cook it, so it'll be waiting."

They laughed again.

When they were rung up, he slipped past her and got his card into the machine before she could stop him. She bumped into him trying, and they both ended up laughing. He was glad to see her having a good time and glad to contribute financially to the day.

After she bumped into him, he held her around the waist. They were in public now. She didn't complain, but she seemed a little self-conscious, if also a little expectant. Unfortunately, he had to release her to help with the cart and the bags.

When they got back home, the boys came out to help them get everything inside. Alex was excited about the games, and Jeremy, looking at the young man, felt foolish for the assumptions that he'd made before. Alex was like an older son to Angelina, and now Jeremy couldn't even imagine them being anything else.

Angelina watched as they moved things inside, clearly wary of the way he'd insinuated himself into her family. But she said nothing and began unpacking the groceries.

"There you are," Aunt Rose said. "Invite the young man to dinner, Angelina."

Angelina rolled her eyes but said very politely, "Would you like to stay for dinner, Jeremy?"

Aunt Rose couldn't see them because they were standing behind her chair, and Angelina shook her head.

"I'd love to. Thank you."

Jeremy helped her start dinner and then spent some time with Aunt Rose and the boys while Angelina finished. He went back in to help set the table, and they had a real family meal together. Phillip filled them in on the games they'd played, with Alex and Aunt Rose adding details.

"When is Phillip's next appointment?" Jeremy asked.

"Not this Tuesday but next Tuesday."

"I'll meet you there."

Angelina had some papers to grade, so after helping with the pots, Jeremy got ready to leave.

"Walk him to the door, honey," Aunt Rose said from the kitchen table.

Angelina rolled her eyes again, but she walked with Jeremy to the front door. Aunt Rose could see them from the table, and under her watchful eye, he gave Angelina a chaste kiss on the lips.

"I think your great-aunt likes me," he teased.

"I know she does," Angelina said. "This is only for her satisfaction."

Jeremy took that as a challenge and pulled Angelina out of the line of Aunt Rose's sight. Alex and Phillip were back at their game and couldn't see them from in front of the television.

He pulled her close to him and kissed her again, this time harder and longer, opening her mouth with his and exploring it with his tongue. He ran his hand up and down her back until he felt her body shiver, and then he pulled her closer to him, lifting her hips just a little to bring her center up to his.

Finally, her arms came around his neck, and her body pressed back against his. When he brought one of his hands to her breast, her lips went soft beneath his, and she held onto his tongue with her mouth, sucking it inward. He wrapped his arms around her and pressed her harder against him. A quiet murmur escaped her throat.

Her own voice seemed to bring her out of the moment. She opened her eyes and looked at him. He kissed her temple where he had kissed it that morning, turned around and headed down the walk to his car.

Jeremy turned on his engine and smiled. His body felt hot, flaring from the taste of Angelina's mouth and the feel of her. And he knew beyond doubt that she had felt it just as much. She might not want to admit it, but they'd gotten inside one another on that cruise, and it wasn't going away. He, for one, was still taken by this woman.

Chapter 17

Angelina was putting notes on the last paper from a student in her class on early African-American history. This one was on the way Black women both resisted and reinforced traditional gender constructs during the racial uplift movement that occurred throughout the Reconstruction Era. It used works by Frances E. W. Harper and Anna Julia Cooper as primary sources and had two additional secondary sources.

It was well written, easy to read and followed the directions. It was a good essay, the kind she lived for. There would be no need to torment herself over the grade—A. She entered the score in her grade book and shut it.

She had papers for her survey of American history to 1865 and paragraphs for her World War I course. At least the paragraphs could get done on Tuesday, her next day off from classes.

She cleared the papers from the center of her desk and was about to pull out the notes for her critical article. But it was almost midnight. She wouldn't get much done before having to turn in. Instead of that, she wrangled her creative writing from the bottom of another pile so that she could reread the last few chapters and at least stay in touch with what she hoped to do.

It was a historical novel about a family of Blacks who owned slaves in South Carolina. They were second-generation slave owners, and the father was also known as a slave breaker. It was supposed to be about all of the ironies involved in being Black and owning slaves.

Ever since the cruise, though, it had started taking on an unexpected romantic subplot. The daughter of the family, who hated slavery and hoped to attend school in the North to get away from it, was falling in love with one of the slaves they owned, an African-born man who'd been sold farther south because he was rebellious. It fit her themes, but she would have to go back and redo her outline to take into consideration this major new plot strand.

Angelina read the last five chapters, the ones she'd written since the cruise. There it was—a plot that she hadn't figured on, coming to life before her eyes. And the more she thought about the romance plot, the more the slave seemed to her like Jeremy: tall and dark, the color of cocoa, with angular lines but a sweet smile and intelligent eyes. She finished and put down the pages, shocked because she realized that she had been seeing the slave as Jeremy in her mind all along.

She wouldn't have time to work on the novel for a little while, but she could rework her outline in between getting other things done. She didn't have time to see Jeremy, either.

That hadn't stopped him from being a presence in her life, though. He'd taken the boys out for a movie and pizza one Saturday, arranging it with them and Aunt Rose while she was running errands. They'd seen an animated movie and had gotten back while she was making dinner for herself and her great-aunt.

He'd also come to see them at Philly's last appointment. He was loitering at the receptionist's desk when she got there, and he joined them in waiting until the call came for Philly to go inside. That was simple enough, because he worked in the same building, but he was also back in the waiting area when they got out. He got a rundown of the latest news from Alex and then kissed her on the forehead before heading back to work.

And today he'd taken the boys and Aunt Rose out for brunch when she had protested that she had to do class prep and grade papers. She'd worried that he'd have a hard time managing Aunt Rose, but Alex helped, and the whole afternoon seemed to have gone off without a hitch. In fact, her great-aunt was delighted to get out of the house, and she couldn't stop raving over the food once she got back.

She was happy for her great-aunt and pleased that she would be able to get a whole set of papers graded, but there was still a problem. All of this was a way to get to her, but she didn't see how it could work out. Meanwhile, her whole family was starting to like Jeremy.

She hadn't forgotten about becoming a joke for his friends or about what he'd accused her of being in his office. But even if those weren't fatal offenses, she still didn't see how she could manage her life with him in it. Even once summer started, there would be summer classes and articles to get done, and she would be trying to squeeze in time for her novel.

Beyond that, Philly had had another seizure two days earlier. He was already on a low dose of anticonvulsants, so he would have to have more follow-up, which meant more trips to the doctor.

How could she have a relationship? She had to put an end to her involvement with Jeremy Bell.

She didn't want to fully admit it; perhaps that was why she'd let herself be carried along. When she was with him, everything she felt on the cruise came back: fluttering in her stomach, throbbing through her heart. And what she had started to feel with him wasn't going away. It had gotten into her like an intravenous drip, and she couldn't bleed it back out. It was the ache of tenderness, of affection, of...

Angelina got up from the desk in her room and went to

the phone. She dialed Safire's number. She hated the idea of getting advice from her younger sister, but this was an area in which Safire had significantly more experience.

After four rings, she hung up. Safire wasn't home, like a regular twenty-three-year-old on a weekend. She'd come by earlier in the week—toting her latest beau—and had dinner with them. She should have talked to her sister then, when Safire had prodded. But at the time Safire's teasing inquiry hadn't inspired confidence. And just as well. She knew what she should do.

As long as she had to be around him, her emotions would show, and she would be susceptible to the way he affected her. She shivered from his fingertips, and she couldn't retain control when his arms were around her. She couldn't stop what she wished or yearned for or felt. That didn't mean that things could work out between them.

Angelina no longer had Jeremy's cell phone number, but she knew where he worked.

That night, she changed and got into bed, ready for the next day but unprepared to dream of a being held by a bold African slave with warm brown eyes.

The next day, she called from her office to see when Jeremy might have time to speak with her, and on Tuesday, when she didn't have to be on campus, she headed across town. She could have done it on the phone, but he would take her more seriously in person, and she needed to get a result.

Dr. Bell could see her in between his appointments that morning. In fact, he called her into his office almost as soon as she had seated herself in the waiting room.

She held her breath through his brief embrace and then extricated herself.

"I won't bother you for very long," she said, taking a seat in the chair facing his desk.

"Is everything okay? Is Phillip okay?"

"Yes, he's fine. You know he had another seizure last week, but he's on the medication. Dr. Carter says that they can adjust it until the seizures stop."

Angelina shook her head as if trying to wake herself up. How had she gotten on this subject?

"Philly is not why I'm here. I needed to speak with you."

"And you don't have my cell phone number?"

"I don't know what I did with it."

"Here, put it in your phone."

"No, that's not why I came."

"Give me your phone," he said, holding out his hand. "I'll put my cell phone and my home phone in it for you."

She held her ground. "No. That's not why I'm here."

"Look, Angelina, whatever happens between us, I hope that at least we'll be friends. You should have my numbers."

"Write them down for me."

He did and then handed her the sheet of paper. Without looking at it, she folded it up and put it in her purse. When he sat looking at her, she knew she finally had his attention.

"What brings you here?"

"Jeremy, you've been wonderful to my family, and they all just adore you."

"But—?"

"But I don't think I should see you anymore."

"Because?"

"I've had a chance to think about it. Whatever could have happened between us is marred by what happened before—by what your friends said and by what you said here."

He started to cut in, and she held up her hand.

"Even without those things, I just don't have the time to see anyone right now. And that's not going to change during the summer, when I have summer classes and research."

"You won't have to teach this summer or any other summer, unless you want to."

"Yes, I do. But that's not the point. The point is that I

can't manage all of this. And I know that you're great with Philly and Alex, but they're young, and they're getting attached, and that's not a good thing if things can't work out between us."

"As I said before, if we're nothing else, then we're friends, Angelina. I—"

"It can't work out, Jeremy. So what can this be for you other than a tryst, really?"

"This is far more than a tryst, and you know it. And I understand that you don't have a lot of time. I haven't interfered with your work, have I?"

"No, you haven't. But there will always be work and home—at least for as long into the future as I can see. You can have someone who doesn't come with all of this responsibility. You should. You like to go out. You have a life. You need a Safire, and I'm not her."

"You can't tell me that you don't have feelings for me."

She didn't quite know what to say to that, but she was not going to go down on a technicality. She clasped her purse against her chest and refused to show what had come to life inside her. He couldn't see that this hurt her, that losing her dream of him, of them, felt like she was ripping off her own arm, like she was losing him all over again. She sat back and crossed her legs, calm and staid.

"I'm not prepared to have feelings for anyone right now."

"Okay," he conceded. "I'll give you time to figure out how you feel, but I'm not going anywhere. If you need some time to get used to the idea, say that. But you can't say you don't want me."

"I don't want time, and I don't want you. This isn't a good idea, and you can't force me into it. I don't have time for games, especially ones I can't win. And this can't work."

"It will if you give it half a chance."

The intercom on his phone beeped, and he picked it up.

"Okay…I'll be right there." He hung up. "I have to see someone now, but I won't be long. Please wait for me."

She said nothing but waited until he left the office before getting to her feet. It hadn't gone at all as she had hoped, and as long as she expected him to concede, she would be out of luck.

She grabbed her purse and headed out of the hospital. If he insisted on coming around, there was little she could do about it. Eventually, he would see that she didn't have time. Eventually, he would get tired.

She got in her car and slammed the door, realizing then how frustrated she was. She hadn't achieved her goal. She hadn't even come near it. He had heard her request and tossed it aside, determined to pursue his own course. What would it take to get through to him?

In the meantime, she had wasted the morning when she had work to get done for the next day. She headed back across town so annoyed—with herself, with Jeremy—that the car felt hot. If he thought he would simply nudge his way in and ignore her protest, he was in for a surprise.

She focused on papers for the afternoon, glad to find that Alex had gone out looking for work.

She stopped when Philly got home from school, followed soon by a disappointed Alex. It was time to get dinner ready, so she let Philly go outside to play for a while as she pulled some chops out of the fridge and got them on the stove.

She got back to grading early, leaving Philly downstairs with Alex and Aunt Rose. When she heard a knock at her bedroom door, she assumed it was one of the boys.

"Come in, sweetie."

"Sweetie?" a deep voice said.

She turned in her chair to find Jeremy looking at her.

"I thought we should finish our conversation, Angelina. I'm sorry I had to interrupt us. They told me I would find you up here and that I could come."

He closed the door behind him and stood looking over her room.

"I don't think it will do any good. Perhaps you should wait for me downstairs. I'll be down in a minute. We can talk in the kitchen."

"Worried about how this might look to your family? I don't think they care, Angelina. I think they want you to be happy."

Instead of turning around, he came toward her and pulled out the other chair at her table. When he was finished looking around her room and reading the titles on her bookshelves, he turned to her, staring. His eyes were dark and brooding, and filled with something she couldn't identify.

"It's okay if they get used to me being up here with you, Angelina."

"I have an example to set, Jeremy."

She stood to walk them both downstairs. Only he also stood, and before she knew what he was going to do, he had crossed the short distance toward her and taken her in his arms, backing her to the bed. He lifted her onto the bed and then followed the line of her body, placing himself above her. His mouth covered hers and muffled her protest.

"Jeremy, we can't."

"I know, my love," he said and buried his tongue inside her mouth.

Against her will, her mouth opened for his, and when his knee nudged her thighs open, they disobeyed her, as well. He tugged at her long skirt, bringing it upward as his hand cupped her rear, bringing her against the thick crease in his pants. Her hips tilted forward, ignoring her command to remain still, and her arms settled around his shoulders, flouting her edict to move away.

With his manhood pressing deliciously against the center of her body, her throat let out a muffled whimper, and her hips ground upward. She breathed in his heady, masculine scent, and all of her thoughts were lost to the virile presence of his body covering hers.

He moved himself up and down along her womanhood, reaching between them to massage her breast. She sucked in her breath and moaned quietly.

Her sound drew a garbled groan from him, and he lifted himself slightly, running his hand down over her upraised skirt to the panties beneath. What he felt there made him inhale sharply and claim her lips again before placing himself back against her.

He pulled himself up onto his elbows, running a hand along her cheek.

"I'm sorry, Angelina. I've been wanting to do this for so long that I couldn't resist. Come home with me tonight. Let me make love to you. You're so wet, so ready. I want you so badly."

With more willpower than she knew she had, Angelina pushed him backward and squirmed from underneath him. Her skirt was hitched up to show her panties, and she tugged it down, trying to regain a semblance of dignity.

"No, I told you this can't work, and now you see why. I can't saunter off in the middle of the evening. And I can't have a strange man up in my bedroom."

"I'm not a strange man, and I would have you home by morning. I think Alex can help with Aunt Rose tonight. But—"

He raised his hand to quell her protest and casually lifted himself from the bed.

"But I said I wouldn't rush you, so I won't. Take some time to get used to the idea of us being together."

He went back to the table and sat down.

"We'll get a little extra help for your great-aunt so that you don't have to worry about taking a night off here and there, and don't put in to teach this summer. I know you'll have articles to work on and Phillip to look after, but that's it."

"Don't give me directions, Jeremy. I'm not going to shirk my responsibilities—"

"No one is saying that, but a little extra help so that we can have some time with each other is a reasonable request, not a direction, and I can afford it. And I can help more than you give me credit for. By the way, when do I get to make the lamb?"

"You're not listening again."

"I'm listening to everything—everything you say and everything you don't say."

"Look—" she started. But he cut her off.

"If I needed a Safire, I'd be out looking for one. What I want is you."

"No. It's just leading us both on when it won't work."

"Think about it, love," he said. He kissed her before heading out the door.

After he was gone, Angelina balled her fists up and pounded them against her thighs. If her body had listened to her, he might have taken her seriously, but she had acted like a wanton hussy, letting him lift her skirt and feel what was underneath.

He thought he wanted to play homemaker, but he had no idea what was involved, and in the meantime Philly and Alex were getting more attached. She herself was getting used to having him underfoot all over again. And she did want him—it was like a toothache. She wanted to play with him in a tropical rainforest and feel his arms about her and get lost in his warm brown eyes. But that was all fantasy.

She had to get a hold on her emotions and do what made sense.

Chapter 18

"Do these go in the dishwasher?" Michelle asked.

"Everything goes in the dishwasher," Jeremy said. "There's nothing it can't handle."

Alistair came into the kitchen. "Thanks for the magnificent eats. Can I help?"

"Nope. Miss Daisy needs no assistance."

"I know you didn't just call me Miss Daisy," Michelle said.

"Miss Daisy is the new dishwasher," Alistair said, and he and Michelle laughed.

"Laugh if you will," Jeremy said, "but Daisy's got it going on."

"You guys go ahead," Michelle said. "I'll find you when I'm done."

In Jeremy's bedroom, Alistair lounged back on the sofa and kicked his knee over the arm. Jeremy took his carry-on out of the closet, opened it on the bed and started tossing items inside.

"Why are you going home?"

"I don't know. I've been spending time with Angelina's family—her brother and cousin and great-aunt. It makes me appreciate having parents who are still around. So I thought I'd go see them, see what trouble Eddy's up to."

"Is she going?"

"No, but I wish she was. My parents are going to love her."

"You sound certain they're going to meet."

"No, just wishful thinking. Any news for your mom?"

"No. Just ask her when she's coming."

"Next month."

"Huh? How do you—? Oh, it's her birthday. Oh, snap. I almost forgot."

"Just tell her I'll see her next month."

"Who?" Michelle asked, plopping down on the bed.

"My mother," Alistair said.

"Any message for your family?"

"No, just say hello for me."

"You know," Jeremy said, "next time we all go together. And I don't mean for Thanksgiving or Christmas."

"Yeah," said Michelle. "Let's go for a week over the summer."

"And I'm bringing Reggie."

"And I'm bringing Angelina."

"And her brother and her cousin and her great-aunt," Alistair said and laughed.

"Actually, yes. It's about the only way I would get her to go, anyway, if she's still talking to me at all."

"Do I hear trouble in paradise?"

"Well, she keeps telling me to get lost, if that's trouble."

Michelle and Alistair laughed, and Jeremy found himself laughing along with them. It was a rather absurd situation. If only he could get her to just give him a chance.

"Oh, and she said that all it could be for me is a tryst."

"Ouch," Michelle said. "Maybe she has your number."

"Trysts can be good," Alistair said. "But—"

"But that isn't what I want with her," Jeremy admitted.

"Could it just be the thrill of the chase?" Michelle asked. "I mean, you've never had to work to get a woman before."

"No, it's not that. I'm really serious about her."

"Is that why you don't listen when she says to get lost?" Michelle asked.

Jeremy sat down on the bed and looked at her. "It's that,

and it's how she responds to me when we're together. That keeps me hoping."

"Well, we'll hope with you," Alistair said.

"Thanks."

The next afternoon, Alistair gave him a ride to the airport so that that he could get home to Houston, Texas. His younger brother, Edward, picked him up because his visit was a surprise for his folks.

Edward was shorter than he was, with big dimples in his grin, which was usually twisted to the side in some bawdy humor. Edward was filled out like he was, athletic like he was, and a lady killer in an Oxford shirt and pleated slacks. He still had childhood hidden in his face, which didn't match his lewd sense of humor and constant pursuit of the ladies, but it helped him with the latter.

"Hey, Biggie," Edward said.

He threw his arms around his older brother and gave him a bear hug, and Jeremy felt as though he was home. He stayed at Edward's overnight and surprised his mother in the morning.

At his parents' house, his mother nearly dropped the bowl of greens that she was carrying when he and Edward walked through the door.

"My goodness," she said. "I nearly had a heart attack. Come in here, honey."

Jeremy's mother was a small woman with an ample figure and delicate manners. For as long as he had known her, she had worn her hair in a tight bun and worn diva hats to church on Sundays. Her dark copper face was always animated, always full of expression. To her sons, it was the face of love.

His mother put her bowl down on the living room table and patted her chest. "I swallowed my chewing gum."

All three of them laughed. Then Jeremy hugged his

mother, picked up the bowl for her, and the three of them went into the kitchen.

"Your father's gone to get a few things from the store. He'll be right back. I'm in here picking greens. If I knew you were coming, I would have had something made already."

"That's the point. I don't want to be any trouble. I just wanted to see you guys. How are you doing? How are Grandma and Gramps?"

"We're all fine, honey. How long are you staying? They'd love to see you."

"I brought a couple of things for them. I'll go see them tomorrow and take them to brunch. You guys up for it?"

"What time is brunch?" Edward asked.

"We know that if you're going, it won't start before two," Jeremy said.

"Stop teasing your brother. You know he'll make it at noon, if need be."

Both Jeremy and his mother laughed. Edward pouted, and Jeremy grabbed Edward's head, wedged it under his arm and rubbed his knuckles over his brother's head.

"Okay, okay," Edward said. "Uncle."

"We're just teasing, little brother." Jeremy let his brother go. "We know how you love your beauty sleep."

"Let's say that we'll meet at noon and go get them. You driving, Eddy?"

"Sure, but call me to wake me up."

Jeremy and his mother laughed again.

They heard his father and quieted down.

"Marilyn, are you in here?"

"I'm in the kitchen, Carl," she yelled back.

"They didn't have the—"

His father got as far at the kitchen door. Then he saw his two sons standing at the dining table and did a double take. He put his bags down on the table and hugged his oldest son.

His father had a little potbelly and an easy smile, and when they were growing up, there wasn't anything he wouldn't do for his sons. The same was still true now. Jeremy had been taller than his father since his early teens, but whenever they were together, he always felt like he was looking up. His father was a hard worker, a calm presence, a good man—maybe the best he knew.

"Where did you come out of?"

His father patted Edward on the back and then went up to his wife. He tickled her ribs until she laughed and then kissed her.

"And you, too. Quiet as a mouse."

The teasing between his parents was always spontaneous and usually comical. Today, Jeremy saw through the humor to the deep and lasting affection between them. It made him wish all the more that Angelina had come with him. It showed him how he wanted to be with her and how he thought they could be together—not the same as his parents but with the same tenderness between them.

He also now understood a bit better what it meant for his parents, both of whom were still working, to look out for his grandparents. His mother's parents were the only ones still alive, and they lived on their own, but his parents—one or both—saw them at least every other day.

Jeremy went back to the living room and pulled a bag out of his carry-on.

"I got some things for you guys on the cruise. Next time, we all have to go together."

He gave his mother the gold rope necklace with the matching earrings, and his father and brother matching mariner-link gold chains. The gold locket was for his grandmother and the watch was for his grandfather. He left those in the bag.

"You've done enough for us already," his mother said.

He'd helped them get a new house and pay it off, but in his mind, that didn't count, not after all they'd done to help him through school.

"It's a good son who thinks of his parents," his father said. "But there's no need to go overboard."

"Are you saving for a rainy day, sweetheart?"

"Always, Mom."

"Oh, they're beautiful, honey," she said, opening the box.

"Thank you, Biggie," Edward said.

"Thank you, son," his father echoed, giving his arm a short squeeze. "Now, what are we going to do with you while you're here?"

"You don't have to do anything with me. It's March Madness. We can stay in and watch the games."

"Or you can come to a new club with your little brother." Edward winked at him.

"That's why you won't get up until noon," Jeremy said and then laughed. "I'll pass this time, but maybe next time. You be careful out there."

"Come on, both of you. Let me show you what I'm doing to the backyard and the garage."

The two brothers looked at each other. Their father was endlessly building something. What was it this time? Jeremy kissed his mother and followed his father down the back porch to the backyard.

After a tour of the new barbeque pit in the yard and the new shelving in the garage, Jeremy's father took them with him to the hardware store for some more building supplies, and they stopped to get some snacks for the game and some extra groceries.

"Next time, tell me you're coming, and I'll get us tickets for a game," his father said.

Jeremy, the tallest of the three men and the older of the two brothers, carried the bag of concrete mix out to the back where his father would use it to finish a wall around the fire pit. He also realized what he'd be getting his parents for Christmas—new patio furniture.

They hung out at home for the afternoon, waiting for the first game to start while his mother cooked. His father would be lighting up the old barbecue that evening. He didn't know that while they were gone, his mother had been on the phone to some neighbors and friends. The house would be packed that night because her eldest son was home.

There were twelve people in the house by the time the game started. His father watched the beginning of the game and then went to start the meat on the barbecue. Jeremy spent the evening getting drinks, refilling snack bowls and watching the game with Edward and a growing group of his parents' friends.

The women who came either joined the group in front of the game or headed to the kitchen to help his mom—except for Amanda, his mother's attempt at matchmaking. She was a neighbor's daughter, and from the moment she hit the door, she made Jeremy her focus. She was nice enough, but she wasn't Angelina, so she didn't stand a chance. And for her, it seemed he was less a person than a means to an end, a means to a nice life, and Jeremy didn't like that feeling.

He spent half of the evening sending her polite signals to leave him alone, and when she cornered him in the dining room, where his mother had set the food out, he finally confessed that he was already interested in someone in Florida.

She looked him up and down, like Safire had, and left his options open. "If it doesn't work out, you'll know who to call."

Near the end of the second game, his brother left to go to the club, and he got up to help his parents start clearing things away. Most of the company had gone, and others took the signal as he gathered up glasses and plates. His father was taking a breather in front of the game, and his mother was still in the kitchen, where she had spent most of the evening.

"I heard you tell Amanda that there's someone you're interested in. Was that just to get her off your case, or is there someone?"

"Are you the one who invited Amanda, Mom?"

He laughed as he said it because he could tell it was true.

"I'm sorry, son. But you know I'd like to see you and your brother settled down before I'm gone. Eddy's just about as bad as you were at that age."

"Okay. He has to come visit me in Florida. I think I have the perfect match for him," he said and laughed, thinking of Safire.

"Don't you go encouraging him. And beware of playing matchmaker like I just did. I won't be doing it again."

"Thank heavens."

He laughed, and then his mother started to laugh.

"It was well intentioned."

"There is someone I'm seriously interested in. But…"

"But what, honey?"

"We hit a couple of bumps, but mainly, she wants to call things off before they really get started because she has too many responsibilities right now."

"Is she worth waiting for?"

"I think so."

"Then give her time. Young people your age are just starting to build their careers, still trying to pay off college loans, still trying to get stable. If you give her time and show her you're there, she'll make time for you."

"I've been trying to do that."

"Good. I raised you right. Now, tell me about her."

Jeremy smiled. Trying to tell someone about Angelina wasn't the easiest thing to do, but he did his best, and his mother started to get the picture.

He felt odd talking to his mother about a woman. This was the first time since medical school that he had reason to mention one to her. It let him know how serious he really was about Angelina—serious enough to talk to his mother about her when she was telling him it wouldn't work out.

It also meant that the stakes were higher if it didn't work out. His mother would be asking. He hoped he would have good news for her.

They finished cleaning up and got to bed—late for his parents but just in time for him. The next morning he called and got his brother up. He heard the muffled sounds of a female voice and had to ask. "Anyone special?"

"Just a friend I met last night."

"Mom's right. I think I have to have a talk with you," he said and then laughed.

"You better not be one to talk, Biggie. Don't forget I got the 4-1-1 on you."

"I know. Just be up front, and be careful."

"I always am."

"You have an hour. Get a move on. Old folks are waiting."

"Okay, okay." Jeremy heard more muffled female sounds. "I might be a few minutes late."

"Don't even think about it. Get a move on."

"See you soon."

After brunch with his grandparents and the rest of his immediate family, Jeremy took his mother for a little clothes shopping and spent the evening with his parents playing dominos and watching television. It was good just to be with them. He made it an early night because he had a morning flight that got him back to Miami in time to unpack and relax for the next day.

If the trip told him anything, it was that Angelina was having a bigger impact than she knew; his desire for her was more serious than he himself had known.

Chapter 19

When her Aunt Rose had the stroke, Angelina was just getting in from work. She spent every day of the next week at her great-aunt's side in the hospital, leaving only to teach her classes and to look out for Philly and Alex. She brought her things to the hospital to work at her great-aunt's side, but it was difficult to concentrate while worrying.

Others stopped in. Alex brought Philly, who had a seizure right there. Safire came twice. Jeremy came several times. But she was the staple—there every day, talking to the doctors, serving as the point of contact.

Aunt Rose never recovered enough to talk, and within the week she was gone.

The next several days passed in a blur. With only a few weeks of school left in the semester, Angelina couldn't afford to be off work. But she still had to take care of the arrangements, and she had to be there to comfort Philly and Alex, especially Philly, who'd known Aunt Rose his whole short life.

Safire helped a bit with the arrangements, and Alex helped with Philly while she had to be away, and Jeremy came by often. But she was the linchpin who made the final plans, notified friends, found the paperwork. She hadn't even had a chance to deal with her own grief.

And she was exhausted. She had been coping with Aunt Rose's care during the day, looking out for the boys in the evening, working at night.

She didn't start to cry until the day of the funeral, and

then she couldn't stop. For the past six years, Aunt Rose had been the only mother figure Angelina had had. She made it through the funeral and to the graveside, but she couldn't stop the tears from flowing down her face, and that was as far as she made it.

When she collapsed, it was as if she were falling from a great height into a soft place; it was almost a relief. She barely remembered being scooped up by strong arms and carried to a car. She barely remembered the sounds of muffled voices or petting Philly's head, telling him that she was all right. She barely remembered the drive, or protesting that she was okay, or being scooped up again and carried inside. She barely remembered curling up on a big bed and crying herself to sleep.

When she woke up, it was getting dark outside, and she was still wearing her black dress. She didn't recognize the room or know how she'd gotten there. It wasn't a hospital. It was a home.

She got up, found the bathroom, washed her face, and went in search of her shoes and purse and whoever was there.

The plush carpet ran from the bedroom to the kitchen, where she found Jeremy in sweatpants in front of the stove turning over steaks.

"I have to get home," she said. "People are coming. People are there already. I need my brush and my shoes. I need my car. I have to go."

Without knowing she would, she started to cry again. And this time she was aware of the arms that lifted her against a hard body and carried her back to the bedroom. Jeremy laid her on the bed and lay down beside her, putting both of his arms around her.

"You don't have to be anywhere. Safire is handling tonight. And Phillip and Alex are just fine. You don't need to do anything but rest."

His hand petting her hair only made her cry harder. Soon she had cried herself to sleep again.

The next time Angelina woke up, it was dark outside and quiet inside. She found her shoes and purse at the foot of the bed. When the door opened, she was sitting on the bed trying to get her bearings. It was Jeremy with a covered tray.

"You're up. Do you want to eat in here or at the dining table?"

She followed him to the dining room, where he started unloading the tray.

"I should get home."

"Here's my phone. Call and check in with Safire to see how things are. And I'll take you whenever you want."

The moment she said hello she started crying, but she didn't let Safire hear her.

"Is everything okay at home?…And Philly and Alex?… Should I come home?…Okay. Call me if you need anything. I have my cell phone…Okay. Bye."

She wiped her eyes. "She said everything's going fine and that Philly is fine. He's in bed for the night. Alex is helping her clean things up."

She sat at the table, eating slowly because she wasn't hungry.

When Jeremy was finished, he sat watching her, making her conscious that she was pushing the food around on her plate.

"Is it okay? You want something else?"

"No, it's delicious. I'm just not hungry. Thank you for making it."

The events of the day were playing through her mind, and she kept coming back to the singing at the funeral of "I Done Done What You Told Me to Do." Tears started to fill her eyes, and she put her hands up to her face as they began to fall.

She felt arms come around her and turned into Jeremy's

embrace. He had stooped beside her chair, and now he knelt down and turned her toward him, encircling her shoulders and pulling her against his chest. Angelina wrapped her arms around his shoulders and let herself cry, her body shaking with sobs. After a while, her tears abated.

"I'm sorry," she said. "I'm making a spectacle."

"There's nothing to be sorry about."

He kissed her forehead and rubbed his cheek along hers, getting wet with her tears. Then he pressed his forehead to hers and rubbed her back as she quieted. With one hand wrapped around her body and the other sunk into her hair, he dipped his head and gently kissed her lips. Then he pulled his lips away and pressed their cheeks together again.

"It's going to be okay, Angelina." He pulled back a little and looked into her eyes. "It's going to be okay."

"I know," she said, but tears still flowed down her face.

In the silence that followed, they moved toward each other at the same time. Their lips met, and their arms tightened about each other. Her resistance was gone. Angelina's lips parted, letting Jeremy's tongue move into her mouth and run along her own.

Angelina felt her heartbreak give way to the desire that was building inside of her. Jeremy's tongue lit the flames of her yearning, and his hands began to run along her back, sending goose bumps over her body. Her hands gripped his arms as heat spread through her middle and down to her thighs.

She found herself moving upward as Jeremy stood, bringing her with him and pulling her body against his. She felt the swelling in his sweats through the weave of her black dress, and it pressed against her center, filling her with need. Her hips leaned toward it, raking her over him. She grew wet and started to throb. She wanted him so much. When he lifted her rear to drag her upward onto him, she moaned in his mouth.

When he broke their kiss, her eyes flew open. He breathed for a moment before he spoke.

"I didn't bring you here to take advantage of your grief." He let out a heavy sigh and wrapped his arms around her shoulders. "I've wanted you for a long time and don't want to stop. But we *should* stop because you need to get some rest."

His deep voice filled her senses, and his lips brushed against her ear as he spoke, sending shivers through her body. Without thinking, she reached for his ear with her tongue, and then her lips reclaimed his mouth.

She was already lost in the sensations coursing through her body when he lifted her and carried her to a different room from the one she woke up in, one more spacious and with a larger bed—his room. He set her down on her feet next to the bed and turned on a night-light. In the dim light of the large room, she suddenly felt vulnerable. Her hands came up to her neck, her forearms covering her chest.

When he came back to her, his arms went around her, but he didn't hold her; instead, he fumbled with the zipper of her dress until he was able to draw it down her spine. He slipped his hands inside, and she felt her body tremble as his fingers moved up and down her back. Then he pulled the dress from her shoulders, drew her hands down from her chest and let the dress fall to the floor. Then he lowered her nylons and beckoned her to step out of them and out of the dress.

The passion in his eyes sent a hot wave into the pit of Angelina's stomach. In only a black bra and panties, she stepped forward and entered the shield of his arms. His hands drew her to his chest and locked her to his hard body. His lips crushed her mouth, making it his own. With a soft groan, he settled her over him, letting her feel it where her body yearned for that sweet pressure.

Pleasure started building inside of her, and her body

ached for more where it made contact with his. She began rubbing herself up and down against him, feeling the moisture building up inside of her. He moaned, pressing his body to hers, and tore his mouth away.

"Angelina, are you sure you want this? Are you sure you want this now?"

She nodded, afraid of giving away the extent of her desire.

He unclipped her bra and sat on the bed, taking one of her breasts into his mouth and stroking it with his tongue until she trembled. He moved to her other breast, pulling her panties down so that his fingers could squeeze her rear and explore her womanhood.

"Angelina, you're so wet, so ready."

He pulled the covers back as he stood, and after she slipped inside, he drew off his clothes and went to the dresser to rifle for a condom. He came back to her already sheathed and got under the covers with her, moving downward until his lips found her breasts. She cried out with pleasure and thrust against his hip, wanting to feel his body against her pulsing sex.

In response, he moved farther down her length, taking her womanhood into his mouth. Angelina moaned as fire licked through her body. Her knees fell apart, and she thrust wildly against his mouth while the pressure built inside her, driving her toward the edge. She moaned and couldn't stop moaning, not with his tongue encircling her sex and making her body flood with moisture, not with his lips suckling her and making her oscillate.

Angelina called Jeremy's name, admitting her desire.

She clenched the sheets as her thighs started to tremble, and when he reached up to massage her breasts, it pushed her over the edge. She cried out again as waves of ecstasy coursed through her body, bursting from her center.

Starting to calm from the sheer excitement of the moment, Angelina felt naked and exposed, as though her body had just made a confession that she didn't want known. The hands that had been gripping the sheets came up across her body, and her eyes flew open. She was aware now of the wild gyrations of her body, and the vision of what she had done so flagrantly made her self-conscious.

Jeremy climbed up next to her and cradled her gently in his arms, brushing her mouth with his lips. He ran his hand through her hair and traced the path of her recent tears with his thumb.

"You're so beautiful, Angelina. I love giving you pleasure."

He pulled her body toward him, drawing his hand up and down her back and over her hip. His adoration of her body with his wandering hand gave her the courage to touch his shoulder then to draw her fingertips along his hard chest and stomach. The soft moan and hard shudder that came from him spurred her to lower her hand. She caressed his leaping member with her fingertips, drawing a hard, involuntary thrust from his body.

They were starting all over again, this time slower, this time more tenderly.

He lifted himself and lowered his body over hers until his manhood nestled between her thighs. He moved over her, teasing her with it until her hips tilted upward as her body sought more contact. His chest raked her breasts. His tongue filled her mouth. Her senses were inundated with his masculine presence.

Angelina felt the pressure building in her and gyrated against the source of her yearning, her sex throbbing.

"Make love to me, Jeremy."

He moaned and drew himself to her entrance, lingering there only long enough to fill her with need. Then he slowly thrust inside of her, and her walls clenched around him. A wave of heat spread through her body, and she met his thrust, crying out in anguish and pleasure.

"Are you okay, Angelina?"

"Yes, yes. Please don't stop."

His hips jerked at her words, and he began to plunge inside of her, filling her with excitement. She clung to his shoulders and moved with him, needing him, needing this, craving this release. She arched her back to draw her breasts along his chest, feeling the nipples turn again into hard, sensitive knobs. She opened her mouth wider, sucking in his tongue.

As his thrusts filled her, her body clamped onto his, pushing her closer and closer to the edge. Their moans called to each other, making music of the passion rising between them.

Jeremy called her name, her real name, and his thrusts became short and hard, plunging her into bliss. Her womanhood tightened around his sex, making him wince and groan, but he didn't stop, and soon Angelina was crying out as the rapture exploded inside of her, dragging her over the precipice.

Jeremy pulled his mouth from hers and called her name again, his thrusts becoming deep and long, his body beginning to shake as his eruption joined hers.

He settled next to her again and took her in his arms.

"I think you've been wanting that as much as I have."

She didn't say anything but continued to stroke the arm that he had placed across her. When she had the courage to look into his face, she could see that he knew it was true.

"I missed you," he said, "and you missed me, too."

She still stroked the arm that held her, unwilling to confess. Then she looked at him and smiled.

"Aunt Rose really liked you."

"I'm glad she did. I liked her, too."

The thought of her great-aunt returned Angelina's sadness, and unexpected tears welled up in her eyes. She didn't want to cry, but she couldn't stop the tears from sliding toward her ear and nose.

Jeremy gathered her closer, settling her naked body against his own.

"I know you miss her."

"I do."

Saying it made it real. She turned her face into Jeremy's shoulder as the tears fell.

"It's okay," he said. "It's going to be okay."

"I know, but I miss her."

"I know."

He held her tightly as the sobs began to shake her body. Angelina felt she was in a place where it was safe to cry—in Jeremy's arms. He rocked her gently as she let the tears fall. He rocked her gently as the weariness overtook her again. He rocked her gently as she felt herself drifting into sleep, warm and naked against his body.

Chapter 20

Jeremy loved having Angelina in his home, even when she was just sleeping in one of his spare bedrooms. Having her in his arms and in his bed was even better; he was beside himself.

When the buzzer rang on Sunday, he jogged to the door, hoping to catch it before it woke his guest. He swung it open without asking who it was. He was expecting Safire, and there she was.

"Hey, you have a Park Avenue address, but it's not easy to find."

"It is once you know this side of town. And it's not Park Avenue."

"Well, it looks like it."

She came in, lugging her sister's carry-on and briefcase, and looked around the living room. Jeremy became aware of the leather sectional, the mahogany dining set, the packed entertainment center and the plush carpet as Safire took everything in.

"Nice digs. Where's big sis?"

"She's still sleeping. I didn't want to wake her. She needs rest."

"I can imagine." She sat down on the sofa. "What can I do?"

"How long can you look after Phillip and Alex?"

"They're no problem. I can stay over tonight and come back after work."

"Can you stay over until Tuesday? I'm going to try to

get Angelina to call in sick tomorrow and stay here. Did you bring her work?"

"Yep, what was on her desk and in her briefcase. I can stay."

"If she agrees to get some rest, I'll bring her home Tuesday evening, and I'll cook the lamb that's in the freezer. Can you put it in the fridge Monday night?"

"Will do. What else?"

Safire pulled her legs up underneath her on the couch and stretched her back, and he saw in her posture and gesture how young she was, how sheltered she had been from the day-to-day worries of her sibling.

"I think that's it. If it's too much, say so, and we can make other plans."

"No, it's fine. I'm taking the boys to a movie this afternoon, and we're going to do a little grocery shopping."

"Here, let me give you some money."

"No, we're okay. But thanks. Hold it for when I want something big."

Jeremy laughed, knowing she would likely call in the favor.

"How is Phillip? Is he taking his medicine?"

"Philly's fine. He misses Angelina a little, but he's making do with me and Alex. Alex is solemn, but he's okay."

"Good. I'm going to get lunch ready for when Angelina wakes up. You want something?"

"No, I should be going. I was just enjoying the ambiance."

Safire got up to go.

"You take care of my sister, you hear?"

She winked at Jeremy, and he got her double meaning. He laughed but said nothing, sure that Angelina would be tight-lipped with her sister about "being taken care of."

"I'm going to have to introduce you to my brother. You all will get along like peas in a pod."

"I'm not sure if that's a compliment, but it sounds like I might like to meet him. Give him my love."

She blew him a kiss at the door and clopped down to her car in her three-inch heels. Jeremy shook his head as she left, still amazed at how well she fit the description in the singles brochure.

When lunch was done, he went into his room to wake up Angelina. He found her naked in his bed and couldn't help smiling. He got onto the bed and played with her hair before kissing her shoulder. She jerked it as if he were a fly she was shooing away, and he laughed. That brought her eyes open.

"Hello, beautiful."

"Hi. What time is it?"

"Time for lunch. I didn't want to wake you earlier, but I think you should eat something."

She pulled the covers up to her neck and looked around for her clothes. They were on a chair next to his side of the bed.

"I'll bring you a robe. You can take a warm bath when we've eaten."

He smoothed her hair and leaned down to kiss her again.

"Are you okay today?"

"Yes, I'm a lot better."

He went to his closet and brought her back a robe. He kissed her shoulder and her neck, and she smiled. Then he held open the robe for her and slipped it over her back.

"Thank you."

"There's a new toothbrush in the bathroom. When you're finished, come get lunch."

She closed the robe around her and emerged from under the covers.

"Okay."

She came out of the bedroom as he was setting the food on the table.

"Your house is amazing."

"I'm glad you like it. I want you to spend more time here. I also have two guest bedrooms, so Phillip and Alex can visit when you do or when you need time to work."

"How do you keep it so clean? Do you have a cleaning service?"

"Yes, I do, though I hate to admit it. They don't have to do a whole lot, but I'd be lost without them. Dig in."

"Aw. My Aunt Rose loved this kind of ham. She wasn't supposed to eat too much of it, but on Christmas and Thanksgiving, she had to have some."

Jeremy heard Angelina's voice waver just a little bit, but she seemed determined not to cry.

"I had some friends over. These are just leftovers."

He took her hand for a moment, wanting to comfort her.

"I'm okay." She smiled briefly and then turned back to the food. "Let's have lunch."

"You don't have to put on a brave face with me. I understand."

"I know. But I can't cry all day. I have to eat and change and get home."

"No, you don't. I had Safire bring over your clothes and books and papers. She's staying with Phillip and Alex until Tuesday evening, when I said I would have you home—after you've gotten some rest. They're going to a movie this afternoon. You can check in with them anytime. But for now, you need some food and some rest."

"I—"

"All your things are here. Once you're rested, you can do some work. Call in tomorrow, take it easy and then do a little catching up. Please."

She took a breath, and he could see her thinking it over.

"You don't have to decide now. Think it over for a while."

"Okay. I'll let you know."

"Have some pasta."

They ate, and then he ran a warm bubble bath for her. Trust Safire to neglect to put in any nightclothes. Jeremy gave Angelina a set of his pajamas and told her to take a long, relaxing bath. While she was doing that, he made up the beds and read at his desk.

When she came out, he put her to bed and popped some popcorn for them. Then they curled up together to watch old movies. She didn't mind having his arm around her, and when he teased her about Safire forgetting her nightclothes, she chuckled.

"She told me to take good care of you, too."

He laughed, and she swatted him.

"And I bet you knew exactly what she meant."

"I did not respond."

"That was very adult of you."

"Why, thank you."

In a few hours, she fell asleep on his shoulder. He settled her on the bed and turned off the television. He read for a little bit and then got up to make them dinner.

She came into the kitchen as he was putting the chicken in the oven.

"Your kitchen is as big as my living room."

They both chuckled at that.

"How are you, sleepyhead?" he asked and kissed her on the temple.

"I'm sorry I fell asleep again. I can't believe how much I've slept in the last two days."

"You needed it. You were exhausted. Have you thought about calling in tomorrow?"

"Will you be able to stay with me if I stay here?"

"If you want me to. Let me make a few calls."

"Okay. But just tomorrow. Tuesday, I'll get up and do more class prep and paper grading. You can bring me home when you get off. Is that okay?"

Happy that she would be staying and wanted him there,

at least for one day, he pulled her to him, ready to kiss her. Instead, he tweaked her nose.

"You're cute in my pajamas."

That made her smile. He wrapped his arms around her and found her lips, kissing her smile until her lips molded onto his. He drew one hand from around her and felt for her breast. He loved the way she shivered when he touched her that way, and she did it again, turning him on.

"If I don't stop," he said, "we're not going to have dinner."

"What's for dinner?"

"Chicken and potatoes in wine sauce."

"That sounds fancy."

"No, it's actually pretty simple."

"Let me check in with Philly before we eat."

She went into the living room and made a long call. She was still on the phone when he came out to check on her. He was about to go back into the kitchen to give her some space, but she waved him over to the couch and let him talk to Phillip and then Alex. Phillip chatted about the action movie they'd seen, but Alex was pretty quiet. Then Alex put Safire on the phone. Jeremy said a few words to her and handed the phone to Angelina so he could check on dinner.

After they ate, and even though it was still early, he changed into pajamas. Angelina didn't want to go right back to bed, so they relaxed on the couch and talked.

Jeremy could still see the sadness in Angelina's face, and he could read it in her quietness, her stillness. Along with that, though, he could see the desire in her coming to life. He could feel it in her reactions to their touches, their kisses. She was finally beginning to let herself respond to him again, trust him again. And this made him soar.

He couldn't keep his hands off her after the way she had excited him in the kitchen, and soon he was making out with her on the couch like a teenage boy.

He carried her to bed not long afterward, and after they made love, she fell asleep in his arms.

They woke in time for her to call in sick for the day and then to call and make sure that Phillip got to school on time.

Jeremy wanted her to get some more rest, but she insisted on reading and prepping for her classes so that the next day could be paper grading.

"I'm sorry I had you stay home. I didn't know I'd be ready to get work done."

She had dressed after making calls and had on the blue capris that Safire had packed for her. She also had her books and papers spread out over the desk in his room. He loved the way she'd taken it over.

"I don't mind at all. I can get some reading done while you work."

They read through the morning. He left her only to shower and get lunch ready, then they slept for a couple of hours and she started grading papers.

When the doorbell rang that evening, she was still grading. He knew it was Alistair because they'd spoken earlier in the day. Alistair and Reggie were coming over with takeout.

They were in the kitchen when she came in.

Angelina and Alistair went toward each other immediately, and he embraced her. "Here's the little one who has Jeremy's head spinning," he said. "I'm so sorry to hear about your great-aunt."

When she stepped back, her eyes were wet, and he wrapped her in his arms again.

"I bet that after what happened on the ship, you never thought you'd see me again," she said, trying to laugh it off but not succeeding.

"Oh, sweetie, it's going to be okay."

"I know it is."

"This is my partner, Reggie."

"Hello."

She held out her hand, but Reggie ignored it and hugged her.

"I'm sorry to intrude," she said. "I just wanted something to drink."

"You're not intruding," said Alistair. "We needed to know if you felt like company or not. Should we stay and eat or go?"

"Company is fine. I need to take a break from grading papers for a little bit. What's for dinner?"

"We brought Chinese."

"I just want to call to check in at home. I'll be right back."

"She's gorgeous," Reggie said to him when she was gone. "And she seems really sweet."

"She is," Jeremy said.

"I can see why you're so taken with her."

"Let's hope I can also get her taken with me."

Dinner was on the table by the time she got back, and she and Alistair resumed their treatment of his foibles, to the great amusement of Reggie. It got her laughing, so he was happy to be the subject of their humor.

After dinner, Alistair and Reggie cut out early, giving them their space. Jeremy was grateful because this was their last night together, at least for now. He started kissing her just as they finished loading the dishwasher. He put in the last plate, which brought him close enough to the nape of her neck that he could smell the floral scent of her hair.

He couldn't resist wrapping his arms around her from behind and locking her to the spot.

"I have to grade papers."

"I know. I won't keep you too, too long."

When he ran his lips over the back of her shoulder, her body squirmed, settling her against the rising swell in his sweats.

"You're incorrigible," she said.

"I love the way your body responds to me. I'm addicted to it. Look."

He ran his lips and tongue over her shoulder again, and though she tried to stay still, she couldn't. She laughed and tried to twist out of his arms, but he held her, bringing one of his hands up to play with her breasts. He heard her intake of breath and felt her ease forward and back, teasing his groin.

With his mouth on her neck and one hand on her breasts, he ran the other up her thighs, wishing she had on a skirt. When his fingers found her center, she murmured and tried to get away again, but he still held her.

"Let me touch you, honey," he whispered against her ear and felt her shiver.

Damn, he was as turned on as he wanted her to be. He had to slow down. But first he wanted these pants off her. She laughed when he lifted her, and her arms went around his neck as he carried her into his room.

Her body was responsive to his touches. Still, there was something in her that wouldn't let go, that wouldn't relax, that wouldn't commit. He didn't push it because Aunt Rose had just died, but he knew now that he would never let her go.

Chapter 21

Angelina finished the last paper just in time to get ready. She was going out with Jeremy that night, only this time it was different; they had set a date in advance.

She showered and tried on the dress that Safire had brought to loan her. It was too low-cut for her tastes and too short—typical Safire. It was a dark red cocktail dress that fit close to her body, especially in the bust, where she was a bit better endowed than her sister. It had two thin straps at the shoulders and ended midthigh.

Thankfully, she had a sheer black bolero shirt that she was wearing over it, and she had one-inch black strappy sandals to go with it. Pleated lace around the bottom hem hung down to the middle of her calves, billowing out around her legs and giving at least the illusion of coverage. It should work out. It still made her feel sexy, and she was surprised to find that she wanted to feel sexy. And look that way, too.

When she got to her room, Safire was sprawled on her bed.

"The shirt ruins the effect. And you need higher heels."

"I like this effect, and we'll be walking. Are you sure you don't mind staying until Philly is in bed?"

"No, we'll be fine. Alex is going to watch him after that, though. I'm going out later with some friends."

"I hate asking Alex to watch him," Angelina said, "but he doesn't seem to mind."

"He doesn't, and neither do I. Besides, how often do you get out?"

"Speaking of which, it's time for me to go."

"Oh, yeah, I came up about fifteen minutes ago to tell you that he's here."

Angelina got a pillow and clapped her sister with it. Safire fell back on the bed, laughing.

When Angelina got downstairs, Jeremy was in the living room with Alex and Philly, talking to Alex. She waved at him briefly and sat down, not wanting to interrupt the conversation if he'd gotten Alex talking.

"...but that's what I really want to do—design video games. I know a little about web design, but it's not really applicable."

"Yes, but there are schools that teach that kind of thing."

"I can't afford school. I don't even have a job right now."

"That doesn't matter. Look online and find out where you can take that kind of program. If you can find out where they're offered and get in, Angelina and I will do the rest."

"Why?"

"Because you have potential, and you're family," Angelina said. "We look out for each other."

Jeremy got up from the sofa. "Find a program, and let me know."

"Okay," Alex said.

Jeremy came to her and took her hand as she got up from the couch. After he hugged her, she got her purse, gave Alex pizza money and hugged Philly before heading out.

"Thank you for getting Alex to talk," she said. "I've been trying to get him to think about school for a long time."

"He has an interest. I think he will."

"And you don't have to offer to pay for it," Angelina added. "I've already figured out how we can do it with what we have and student loans."

"We can argue about that later," Jeremy said. "Let's let him get in first."

He took her hand and guided her toward his car, and they

drove to Little Haiti. After they parked, he took her hand again as they started to walk the neighborhood.

"You look beautiful tonight," he said.

"It's one of Safire's dresses. I don't own anything like this."

"It's not your dress that makes you look beautiful, but I like it. I like when you let yourself be sensual."

Angelina could feel her cheeks grow warm, but she couldn't help smiling.

"I think I'll take you shopping one day for some of your own."

"That won't be necessary."

"But it could be fun."

She shrugged, thinking about it.

As they wandered through Little Haiti, Angelina started to relax and enjoy the night. They found a restaurant and had Haitian food, and then they walked a bit more.

"Oh, let's go in here," Angelina said, dragging Jeremy toward a little art shop.

"What did you see?"

"Just everything—the painting, the sculpture. Look at this one."

She pointed to a painting of a little girl in a boat.

"You like it?"

"Not to have, but to see. She's adorable."

There was beadwork in the back—art pieces and jewelry. Jeremy tapped her shoulder and pointed to an elaborate coral necklace with a matching headpiece.

"It's a bit much," she said.

They both chuckled. It would take a diva to carry it off.

"This reminds me of the art store we found in Old San Juan," he said.

"Me too. I think that's one of the reasons I wanted to come in."

In the end, Jeremy got Angelina a small wooden statue

as a keepsake, and they continued their walk around Little Haiti, his arm wrapped around her.

"Can I call you Angie?" Jeremy asked as they turned a corner.

"Only Philly calls me Angie."

"I've heard. Can I call you Angie, too?"

She pursed her lips, unsure.

"I don't know. It started when Philly was little and couldn't say Angelina all at once. It's kind of his special name for me."

"If you really mind, I won't."

Her brow wrinkled in thought.

"Okay. You can call me Angie—sometimes. But don't start a trend."

They found a little ice cream place that had unique island flavors and stopped for dessert. She tried soursop, and he had guava.

Back in the car, Jeremy looked at his watch.

"It's eight-thirty," he said. "What would you like to do now?"

"I know what we can do," Angelina said. "We're near Morningside, right? Let's go the park and watch the sunset over the water. Can you do that at this time?"

"I don't see why not."

They drove to Morningside Park and walked along the waterfront. One of the fields still had a game going on, and there were a few evening runners still out, but they found an empty bench facing the water. Jeremy put his arm around her, and she rested her head on his shoulder.

"We're just in time," she said.

"What?"

She looked up and found his eyes on her rather than the horizon. She pointed to the sky blanketing the water. "For the sunset—we're just in time."

He drew his eyes from her and turned toward the water.

"It's beautiful, but not as beautiful as you are."

She looked up to find him watching her again. She smiled and returned her attention to the colors of the sky.

"I feel like I'm on a vacation. I never do stuff like this."

"Maybe it's time that you do. Maybe you just needed the right company."

She eyed him mischievously for a moment and then bounced her thigh against his. "I don't know that you're the right company. You're probably a bad influence."

In response, he tickled her ribs until she laughed.

"Okay," she said. "I was kidding."

Her legs were crossed in front of her, and he lifted them up and brought them over his thigh, drawing her toward him.

"Do you mind?" he asked.

"No, I'm still comfortable."

As she watched the sunset, he traced lines on her calves and thighs through the lace flaring from her skirt. Angelina unclipped her barrette, shook her hair free and replaced her head on his shoulder. Jeremy kept tracing lines along her legs with one hand, but the other hand, which had been drawn over her shoulder, soon found its way into her hair and began rubbing her scalp.

"You would be a wonderful piano player," she mused.

"Why do you say that?"

"Because you can do two different things with your hands at the same time. It's like patting your stomach and rubbing your head simultaneously. It's not easy."

He was laughing before she had finished.

"You notice everything, don't you? I've always been ambidextrous."

"See," Angelina said, "you'd be excellent with an instrument."

"Should we get a piano?" Jeremy asked. "Phillip can take lessons."

Angelina caught Jeremy's reference to a future for them together and decided to play along.

"It depends. Are we living in your house or mine?"

"Whichever you prefer, but your house needs a little work."

"Tell me about it," she said. "When I win the lottery, I'm going to remodel the whole thing."

"What difference does it make where we live?"

"Your place needs a brand-new baby grand. Mine needs a used upright."

"I can see that. Maybe we should get a new place in between," he offered. "Someplace in between our two jobs so we can both get to work."

"Maybe. I'd love to live on a houseboat."

"You *are* on vacation, aren't you?"

She caught the joke and swatted at him playfully.

"I'm just teasing," he said. "We can look into a houseboat. Can Phillip swim?"

"Yes, he can. But I wouldn't actually trust raising a child on the water. I love the water, though."

"I've seen you swim. I can tell."

"Yes, you've seen me swim in Safire's bathing suit. What was I thinking?"

"You looked beautiful in it."

Before she could respond, he bent his head and pressed his lips against hers. His fist locked in her hair, holding her in his kiss. His other hand left the lace and traveled up to her hip. He pulled her even closer against his chest and parted her lips beneath his. He moved his hand to her chest, and a hot wave washed through her stomach and into her loins.

Angelina didn't know how long they had kissed, but when they pulled apart, the sunset had gone from a dark red streak across the sky to a light blue strip above the water.

"It's starting to get dark," she said.

"Ready to head back?"

She nodded, and they pulled apart. They stood, stretched and walked along the water back to the car.

"Where to now, my love?" he said once they were inside.

"Can I go home with you for a little while?" she asked.

It was tantamount to a confession that she wanted them to make love, and it made her feel a little shy, but she was starting to shed that with Jeremy. It had been almost two weeks since she had spent time at his home, two weeks since they had been together alone. She did want him.

"I'd like that," he said and took her hand.

They were quiet for the first time that night, his fingers woven with hers. The gentle caress sent warm tingles through her body, starting an electricity between them that ran to the pit of her stomach and made it flutter.

Once they were inside, he closed the door behind them and turned to her. His eyes told her that he wanted her as much as she wanted him, and she stepped toward him. Then his soft lips arrested her, sending a thrill into her body, as his lips had always done.

When they broke, he tugged her toward the couch.

"Can I get you something to drink?"

"No, I'm fine."

He sat down and pulled her onto his lap. She felt a bit silly sitting there, but then he pulled her face toward his and found her lips, and she didn't feel anything anymore except the sparks that were going off between them.

His hands worked their way underneath her bolero jacket and began to toy with her breasts, rubbing her nipples into hard peaks beneath the stiff fabric of the dress and bra. Her upper body swayed against his palms, and heat shot through her sex, which started to pulse.

She moved her hand between them into his lap and felt along the ridge in his pants. He moaned and stirred beneath her.

"Do you want me?" he asked.

His attention drew her mind to what she was doing, and she withdrew her hand.

"Don't go away. I want you there."

She moved her hand back between them and began tracing the outline of his manhood again.

"I love when you do that. I just wanted to hear you say that you want me."

Their foreheads were pressed together, and she could feel his eyes on her face.

"Don't you want me, Angelina?"

His mouth was near her ear, and his deep voice sent a shiver down her spine.

In response, she kissed him hard, sucking his tongue into her mouth, and she squeezed her fingers along his sex until it leaped against her palm. Then she nodded. "I do, Jeremy."

He murmured and took one of his hands from her breasts. He ran it along her legs underneath the lace of her gown and up over her closed thighs. When he reached her center, he nudged apart her legs and began to massage her through the thin mesh that covered her. Her sex throbbed harder, and her body bucked under the attention. The stirring inside her released her voice.

"Would you like my lips here?" Jeremy asked.

He tweaked his thumb over her throbbing bud, making her back arch and her eyes flutter closed. She couldn't think, and she could barely breathe as firecrackers went off throughout her.

"Yes."

The world slanted, and Angelina found herself toppled gently onto the couch with the lace of her skirt thrown up onto her midriff and the bottom hem of the dress scrunched up under her open thighs. Then Jeremy's hot mouth was upon her, scorching circles through her panties and suckling her through the slick mesh.

She moaned as the heat of his mouth licked the flames already built up inside her and pushed her to the edge. He tugged at her panties, but she stopped him; she couldn't bear the separation of his mouth from her body. She was already pulsing heavily, already beginning to tighten. She held his head pressed against her center and called out his name. Her thighs began to tremble as waves of euphoria contracted through her.

When she opened her eyes, he was leaning toward her and smiling a silly, triumphant grin that she hated and loved.

She reached for his arms and pulled herself upright, determined to remove the smirk from his face. She stood and reached up under her dress, pulling her panties down and stepping out of them. She had some Safire in her yet.

Angelina straddled Jeremy on the couch and saw his eyes fly open and his expression turn into a look of pure desire. She reached into his back pocket for his wallet and found a condom, unzipped his pants and handed it to him, a look of daring in her eyes. She felt daring tonight.

When she lifted herself over his thighs and settled down onto him, a deep growl started in his chest and poured through his mouth.

He winced, and his thighs thrust him upward to meet her.

"I've wanted this all night," he said.

She began to rock over his thighs, and he moaned again, thrusting with her.

Filled with his hard member, Angelina felt herself growing hotter and wetter, felt flooded with joy. She closed her eyes, held his shoulders and lunged, latching on to his lips to stop herself from breaking apart.

"Wait, wait."

Her eyes flew open. "What?"

He lifted her onto his body and stood.

"I want this to last, and I won't last this way. You're too beautiful."

He smiled at her and kissed her and then strode into the master bedroom. Still inside of her, he laid her gently on the bed.

"It's going to be late when I get you home."

"That's okay."

"Is it?"

"Yes."

Chapter 22

Jeremy moved his sunglasses onto the crown of his head and patted Phillip's shoulder. "It's all right. She won't bite."

Phillip edged toward the pool and bent down to pet the dolphin that had come up to them.

He turned to Jeremy with a smile of triumph. "It's smooth and wet."

The trainer standing nearby whistled, and the dolphin dove upward and flipped back into the water. Phillip squealed as the fine mist from the splash hit them.

They were at the Miami Seaquarium on Virginia Key on a Saturday.

"Okay," said Alex, "enough of the touchy-feely thing. Now it's time for the shark feeding."

"You ready, Phillip?" Jeremy asked.

"Okay."

"Call Safire," he said to Alex, "and we can go to see the sharks. You can collect data for a video game where someone gets eaten."

"Exactly!" said Alex, waving for Safire to come down from the stands.

Safire hadn't worn practical shoes, and while she was tottering down the steps toward them, Jeremy lingered with Phillip and Alex, watching the dolphins at play.

"I've thought more about school," said Alex.

"Good," Jeremy said. "Have you found one that teaches programming for video games?"

"I found an online art school that offers a bachelor of

science in game art and design. It also has media arts and animation."

"Nothing you can actually go to?"

"Yeah, there are a few kind of close—mainly in Tampa and Fort Lauderdale."

"You're not limited to Florida. We'll go with you to get you settled if you move to another state. But Fort Lauderdale isn't too far. You'll need a car so you can bring your laundry home on the weekends. Anywhere you want to go that you can get in, we'll pay. So look for the best school, the best program, not just the closest ones."

"I was thinking I could start out online—get a feel for some of it—then transfer."

"That's fine too."

Safire approached them, her heels ticking against the poolside tiles. Alex quieted, as he always did when Safire or Angelina was at hand.

Safire stopped with her hands on her hips, looking impish in her miniskirt. "Where to next?"

"Sharks!" said Philly and Alex together.

Safire laughed, flung her arms open, and headed down the walk. "Then let's go."

"Are you up to it in those heels?" Jeremy asked.

"Yeah, I'm fine. I was mainly resting from the sun. It feels like ninety degrees."

It was in the low to mid-eighties, so Jeremy wasn't sure whether she was telling the truth or hiding chafed feet. They'd been at it for several hours, though, so he decided that they would call it day after the sharks, just in case.

At the shark feeding, both Phillip and Alex were awestruck and animated. Safire lifted Phillip onto her hip for a better view, but Jeremy offered to take him, and they switched. Phillip didn't seem to mind or much notice.

Safire looked up at him and smiled. "They're used to you."

"I guess so."

"That's a good thing."

After the shark feeding, they strolled back to the parking area. On the way, Jeremy thought to call Angelina to see about dinner.

"Hello, beautiful...No, we're just heading to the car. We were wondering if we should pick up dinner...No, we'll get something...Sure. See you in a little while...Bye."

"What should we get for dinner?" Safire asked.

"McDonald's," Phillip said.

"Chinese," Alex said.

"Let's order out at Dwight's," Jeremy said, opting for a real sit-down restaurant.

Angelina hung up the phone and turned back to her last two papers of the semester. Finals were objective questions, so grading those would be easy. She was feeling lighter already, and she didn't even have to cook dinner that night.

She put a score on the last paper in time to freshen up and set the table before the door opened. In poured Philly, Alex, Safire and Jeremy.

Before she could say hello, Philly launched in, giving her a rundown of the sights at the Seaquarium and all that they had done that day.

"What were the things we petted?" He turned to Alex.

"The dolphins."

"No, no, before that."

"Sea lions."

"Yes, we petted the sea lions, and then..."

Jeremy bent toward her and gave her a brief hug and a hello kiss that made her smile. She was well aware that Safire was taking in the scene and speculating on the extent of their relationship, but she ignored her sister and enjoyed the warmth. She was starting to get used to his affection around her family.

"…have huge throats and just gulp down the meat."

"Bloody fish chunks," Alex said. "It was great."

"Inspiration for the future artist," Jeremy said.

"I'm glad you both enjoyed it. What about you?" Angelina turned to her sister and tugged at her camisole.

Safire was pulling containers of food out of bags and putting them on the place settings. "I had a great time. It was a bit hot, but other than that, I enjoyed it."

"Don't tell me you met someone."

Both of the sisters laughed.

"That's not the only way I enjoy my time."

"Could've fooled me."

The sisters laughed again but then straightened and curbed their mirth. Alex might understand, or rather, surely he had. And Jeremy was there with a silent smirk on his face. Angelina didn't know what had gotten into her—other than the joy of the last paper turned down on the pile, complete.

But it wasn't just that. Jeremy had convinced her to teach only one class that summer, so she didn't have a panic coming up. Philly hadn't had another seizure in a while, and Alex was even looking into schools and programs. Safire and Alex had been great about helping out more with Philly, and all three seemed to like Jeremy. She still missed her great-aunt, but things were going well. She felt a little like celebrating.

"Hey, Jeremy, I only have one more week of classes left, then finals. Do you want to do something next weekend?"

Jeremy kissed her temple as he took the seat next to her. "Do we have to wait?"

"No time like the present," Safire added.

"I can watch Philly," offered Alex.

"And I can stay over so that you don't have to worry." Safire winked at her, and she understood.

Jeremy looked at her seriously. "Only if you got enough done today so that you're not stressed tomorrow."

She nodded.

Jeremy reached over her head, and Safire high-fived him. All three of them laughed.

"Where should we go?" Jeremy asked. "Where haven't you been in Miami?"

"Almost anywhere," Safire replied.

Angelina opened her mouth to protest but then conceded, "Almost anywhere."

After dinner, Angelina changed and packed an overnight bag. She hugged Alex, Safire and Philly, and then she and Jeremy walked hand in hand to his car. It felt like an adventure. She was feeling freer than she ever had—at least on land.

Jeremy got into the driver's seat and leaned over to kiss Angelina the way he had wanted to since he first saw her that day at noon. They had decided to go to Little Havana to listen to some Cuban music and have dessert.

They found a restaurant with live music and ordered *pastelitos* and a *quesillo,* sharing both of them. He watched as Angelina plopped one of the bite-sized pastries into her mouth and found himself captivated by her full, soft lips.

She went after the desserts without restraint, touching his arm in a way that was making his body begin to respond. She leaned toward him, and he caught the scent of her perfume. Something about her tonight was tending toward abandon.

When she realized that her hand was on his arm, she smiled and pulled it back.

"I don't mind."

In response, she placed her hand in his and let her body begin to sway to the bolero that the band was playing. Her torso drifted in the turquoise cocktail dress she had changed into. He could see the swell of her breasts shift under the sheer fabric of the top she wore over the gown, and his mouth began to water—not for the sweets in front of them but for the taste of her skin. She had no idea what her mood was doing to him.

He was about to ask her something when she stood, circled her chair, and with a mischievous grin on her face, held out her hand to him.

"Dance with me, Jeremy."

He was surprised not by her request but by the hint of seduction in her eyes. He smiled, stood, cupped her waist with his hand and drew her onto the dance floor. She spread her palms over his shoulders and slipped them around his neck before bringing her chest against his. For a moment, she rubbed against him ever so slightly. Then she settled into his embrace and began to sway.

He had never seen her this way—this unconstrained, this frisky. It sent a fire through his groin. Of course, it didn't help that he could feel his body pressing against hers in all the right places. He had to stop himself from grasping her behind and bringing her into full contact, at least in public.

The music swung into an upbeat salsa, and she seemed disturbed, not by the music but by the imminent loss of physical contact with him.

"Are you up for this?" he asked.

She held his hand, pushed back from his chest, and did a few salsa steps. "I know a little. You game?"

"Hell, yes." He matched his steps to hers, and she flung her head back and laughed.

"I can't believe I'm doing this," she almost squealed.

"It looks good on you."

And it did. As her hips oscillated to the music, the hem of her dress caressed her thighs, and when she lifted her arm in a spin, her breasts thrust upward. Her whole body was beckoning him, but not as much as the buoyant smile on her face and the sheer spontaneity of her movement.

When the set ended, she was breathless, and so was he. She was taken by the music and the moment. He was taken by her frame of mind and her beauty.

"Let's go home," she said.

It was how she said it and the way she looked him in the eyes that made him hold his breath and count to ten so that he wouldn't tear out of the club without first stopping to pay their tab.

"I have something for you," he said, releasing her hand, as he closed his door behind them.

"Something for me?"

"Yes. It just came, and I can't wait to give it to you." He drew her to the sofa. "Here, sit down."

Jeremy set the large package down in front of her and leaned it against the coffee table, watching the puzzled expression on her face.

"What's this?"

"Open it, love."

As she tore off the first strip of brown paper, recognition spread over her face. Then tears came into her eyes.

"Oh, I love it. Thank you."

He sat down next to her and put his arm around her shoulder. "You seemed to love it when we first saw it. Tell me why."

Angelina felt her heart filling up and spilling over, like her eyes were about to do. It was the painting she'd kept going back to when they were sightseeing in Puerto Rico, the one of the old local couple with a basket of orchids.

"Why do you like it so much?" Jeremy asked again.

Having to say it made her feel even more as though she was about to cry. She took a breath.

"It reminds me of my parents. I don't know why. It

makes me think of them growing older together, or what it might have been like if they could have."

She pawed at the tears running down her face. Some seductress she turned out to be. She placed her head on Jeremy's shoulder and stared at the painting.

She'd been in high spirits all night. School was almost over, and she was feeling liberated already. In fact, she was out on a Saturday night. She had a life. She had set out to pull a Safire tonight, was even wearing one of Safire's dresses that she'd kept from the cruise.

And she'd been wanting Jeremy all evening. The way it felt to move against his body, the way she felt when he turned her in his arms—it had made her randy and even more determined to have a little Safire in her life.

Now, sitting in front of the painting, she was reduced to a sentimental, sniveling idiot. She had already fallen for this man, and now, as if to enchain her heart forever, he had touched her soul. But these feelings didn't dampen the fire that had been lit earlier. She still wanted this man, now even more than before. She turned toward Jeremy and pulled his face down to hers.

Her kiss, first tender, soon became heated. She pulled his tongue into her mouth and opened herself to its onslaught. Soon, her hands were tugging apart the buttons of his shirt and moving across his chest. She moved her lips to his neck, letting his masculine scent fill her head.

When she dipped her head down to the hard wall of his chest, Jeremy winced and shifted on the couch. She felt his fingers caressing her through the thin lace weave of her panties. She couldn't help cupping her fingers over his and pressing them harder against her. She couldn't help reaching toward him and gripping him through the obtrusive layering of his pants. She couldn't help loving this man.

Jeremy stirred between them to undo his buckle, and the distraction brought Angelina back to her senses. With

the sanity that she had left, she rose and took his hand and
led him to the bedroom, where she finished what he had
started. She drew him onto the bed and backed him up
against the headboard. Then she watched him gaze upon
her as she took off her clothes, his eyes painting her with
his desire.

She straddled his thighs, and they kissed. But she needed
him inside of her, and from the looks of him, that was where
he wanted and needed to be, too. She gripped him and lowered herself onto him and felt a thrill flood her.

His hands found her breasts, and Angelina had to grasp
the headboard to steady herself. Then she rode against him,
filling herself over and over with him. The pressure built
inside of her and the heat of his body rose through her to
claim her body. Lost in passion, she blurted out his name.
Then out tumbled a confession she hadn't known she would
make.

"I love you."

Had she said that? Her eyes flew open.

Jeremy's eyes were closed, and his lips reclaimed hers.
Perhaps he hadn't heard. He sucked in his breath and pulled
her roughly against his chest.

"Angelina," he said, but nothing more.

His arms were around her, anchoring her to the movement of his body, filling her with him until she was lost
again in the throbbing within her body.

"Angelina," he called, rocking faster.

He began to shiver just as she felt spasms tearing her
from her senses, just as she lost all control and thrust and
clutched and whimpered.

His moan joined hers, and his body went taut against
hers as he erupted.

Angelina giggled, and Jeremy drew his fingers across
her stomach, making her giggle more.

"What?" Jeremy asked.

He cupped her face, drawing tiny circles along her cheek with his thumb, lost in the beauty of her features.

"We didn't last very long that time, did we?"

Jeremy smiled. It was true.

"It's hard to last long with you," he said.

Angelina, curled against Jeremy's chest, was filled with peace. But Jeremy wasn't calm at all. A thousand thoughts raced through his mind, and jubilation filled him. But he had to know...

"Did you mean it?"

She was quiet. She knew what he meant; he had heard her. She couldn't pretend.

"Yes."

Tenderness filled Jeremy until he thought he would burst. He slid from underneath Angelina and pinned her to the bed with a kiss.

"I love you, too," he said. He saw Angelina's breath get caught in her throat. "I've loved you since before I knew your name. Angelina, marry me."

She thought her ears were betraying her.

"What?"

"Marry me."

Angelina looked into Jeremy's eyes and saw his emotions, his seriousness, his beauty. It drew a confession from her that she hadn't known she was ready to make—another one.

"You know, you've become a character in my novel."

Jeremy pulled himself up onto his elbow. "You're writing a novel? About what?"

"A historical fiction from a history teacher. It's about a rebellious slave who turns out to be a beautiful man. He turns out to be you."

"Will you let me read it?"

"If I ever finish it. If it's any good."

"I'm sure it will be."

They both knew that he was waiting.

Angelina turned toward Jeremy and kissed him.

"Is this my answer?"

"Yes, it is. Yes, I'll marry you."

Jeremy pulled Angelina against his chest and claimed her as his own with his lips.

"That's good," he said, "because there might be a little one on the way."

"What?" she asked.

"We didn't use anything."

"I am," Angelina said. "I mean, I did."

The look of disappointment on Jeremy's face churned Angelina's heart.

"Soon," she said, "but not right away."

"I'll accept soon," he said. "I love you."

This time, when they kissed, it was slow and tempered, as filled with tenderness as it was with passion. But it was building another fire between them. They both knew that they would be making love again, that it had already started—their joining, their life together. And this time, it would last and last.

* * * * *